Tug-of-War

Tug-of-War

JUDITH SOMBORAC

TUG-OF-WAR

iUniverse books may be ordered through booksellers or by contacting:

iUniverse
1663 Liberty Drive
Bloomington, IN 47403
www.iuniverse.com
1-800-Authors (1-800-288-4677)

Because of the dynamic nature of the Internet, any web addresses or links contained in this book may have changed since publication and may no longer be valid. The views expressed in this work are solely those of the author and do not necessarily reflect the views of the publisher, and the publisher hereby disclaims any responsibility for them.

Any people depicted in stock imagery provided by Thinkstock are models, and such images are being used for illustrative purposes only.
Certain stock imagery © Thinkstock.

ISBN: 978-1-4917-4468-0 (sc)
ISBN: 978-1-4917-4470-3 (hc)
ISBN: 978-1-4917-4469-7 (e)

Printed in the United States of America.

iUniverse rev. date: 09/17/2014

For my children: Kristin, Stefan, Natasha and Serge. Appreciate the culture of your past. Know the adversity, privation and strengths of your ancestors. Be grateful for the time and country you live in where life is privileged.

CONTENTS

ACKNOWLEDGMENTS

MANY THANKS TO KURT KNEIDINGER FOR EDITING MY German phrases. And to the late Paul Pavlovich and his daughter, Helena, who read the manuscript early on. Paul and Helena edited the Serbian phrases and gave me valuable feedback about the Serbian culture and encouragement to continue writing. It was such a benefit to have these three people to call on for help to make the book authentic. Thanks also to Milan Somborac for the stories and the inspirations. Without him, the book would not have been written.

FOREWORD

THIS STORY TAKES PLACE IN GERMAN-OCCUPIED SERBIA during four years (1941–1945) of the Second World War. During the German occupation, two local political forces, the Royalist Chetniks and the Communist Partisans, started their guerrilla operations. Militias roamed the countryside terrorizing the population and the country experienced a breakdown of law and order. The German Nazis caused severe hardships for the local people. In Serb-occupied lands, the Germans decreed that a hundred Serbs were to be shot in retaliation for one German soldier killed. Sometimes the Germans would hang or shoot indiscriminately, and sometimes select only males. With the escalating atrocities of war, the Partisans gained widespread approval and support. Serbs came to view this party as their only option for survival, and gave them backing in secretive ways.

Dozens of Yugoslav cities and towns were bombed, many repeatedly, by the Allies (United States Army Air Force, Royal Air Force and Balkan Air Force). The air attacks, among other things, were intended to give support for the Partisan operations, but some of the attacks caused significant civilian casualties.

Tug-of-War is based on true events and the lives of real people who lived in Serbia during these stressful times. The characters have been fictionalized and woven into the fabric of the harrowing truth of the war years.

CHAPTER 1

Bela Palanka, Serbia
June 1942

MIRIANA SNAPPED BACK THE PAGE, PRESSED HER BOOK flat with the heel of her hand, and started the chapter again—for the third time. This time, she would learn it.

Her bed was firm and warm beneath her, a comfortable old friend. She was 15 now, and it was the first and only bed she had slept on since leaving her crib. She stretched her lean body and curled up again, resting her head on the palm of her hand and feeling her elbow press into the mattress. The whirr of the mill outside made her feel sleepy.

Read, Miriana commanded herself. *You have a test Monday. You have only the weekend to learn this.*

She riveted her eyes on the words one by one, pronouncing each one silently, but her mind kept slipping back to school that day. It was a tug-of-war between studying and the memory of her embarrassment in class. A hank of her medium brown, bushy hair slid like a snake across her cheek and over her shoulder until, finally, it fell across the page, obscuring the words.

Miriana moaned, slamming the book shut. She swung her feet onto the small mat and padded across the wooden floor in her bare feet to the dresser.

The water-powered wheel of the gristmill creaked and hummed as it turned a massive millstone housed in an old, wooden building, grey with age and neglect. When the whirring stopped, she could hear her mother working in the kitchen adjacent to her bedroom. Miriana recognized the clink of dishes and the tinkle of cutlery.

Mama must be preparing supper, she thought, with a pang of guilt. She knew her mother had been working side by side with her father all day at the dual-purpose saw and gristmill, and she knew she should be helping with dinner.

Miriana picked up her hairbrush by its elaborate metal handle and stroked her bushy hair back from her face with one hand. With the other, she held the springy clump in a ponytail. She exchanged the brush for a ribbon and wound it round and round until she could tie it in a bow. As usual, some strands of hair came free, and she stabbed at them with some hairpins.

"Miriana!" she heard her mother calling from the kitchen.

"Coming, Mama," she replied, grabbing a few more pins and picking up the hand mirror that matched the brush to inspect the job.

The dresser set was Miriana's treasure. She had been very fond of her grandmother, Baba. When she was a little girl, Baba had brushed Miriana's hair with this brush every day while Miriana stood in front of the mirror, following her moves with her eyes and feeling the tenderness of the strokes.

A pain. My hair is such a pain, she thought as she secured two more bushy locks that had escaped the tenure of the ribbon.

The reflection of her eyes flicked around the mirror until they were satisfied the job was done and they came to rest, staring back at her. Her eyes were almond-shaped, light grey, and almost green under thick, curved brows.

Her skin was smooth, clear, and pale, her broad, Slavic cheeks showing just a hint of peach. She composed the line mentally, practising and noting the description for her writer's notebook. Her teacher thought writing was her forte.

Her teacher! She would never understand him. At the thought of school, she blushed, and the embarrassment she experienced returned. She wondered how Stefan was feeling. Sometimes Mr. Josich was so encouraging. But today, when he had intercepted the note Stefan tried to send to her in class, he had been rude. Stefan, her best friend, lived on a farm not far from her parents' property. They had been close friends for so long, Miriana knew the note must be important or he wouldn't take the risk in class.

It had been Olga's fault. Ugly Olga. She had drawn Mr. Josich's attention to the note. Mr. Josich's face had grown red, and sharp words tumbled from his mouth. Miriana clasped her hands over her ears, burning at the memory. All day, this uneasiness had stayed with her, intruding in her thoughts and causing her stomach to be queasy.

There was a sharp knock at her door, and Miriana's mother's tired face peered in.

"Miriana, what's taking you so long?" she queried.

"I'm coming, Mama. I was just combing my hair," Miriana replied. Carefully, she replaced the brush and hand mirror on the dresser top and followed her mother into the kitchen.

From the square window, Miriana could see her father washing up at the pump in the yard. A stream of water splashed over his thick, burly body and his balding head with its fringe of black curls. He pumped vigorously for a minute with strong, hairy arms, and when the water stopped gushing, he groped blindly for the towel hung askew on a nail on the shed. He reminded Miriana of a bear—strong and gruff—even when he meant to be gentle.

"Miriana, where is your head today?" Mama asked, without looking up from her work. "Set the table."

Miriana counted out plain, worn cutlery and chipped, ceramic white dishes for three and placed them on the oak table. The table, hefty and worn, sat squarely in the centre of the small kitchen eating area. On one side, a sturdy, bulky bench, also hewn from local oak trees, spanned the length of the table. On the remaining sides, four carved wooden chairs with hearts turned in the wood of the backrests filled the space. The old furniture, passed on through at least three generations on her father's side, reminded her of her father.

Built just like Tata, she mused.

Miriana could smell salami and ripe cheese, but even those sharp odours did not pique her appetite. Just as Mama finished the salad, Miriana heard her father's heavy footsteps on the stoop. The screen door squeaked open as he entered and then slammed shut behind him. It always banged if you didn't take time to hold it while it closed.

Tata gave Miriana a rough kiss, his whiskers scratching the soft skin of her cheek, and took his place, wordlessly, at the table.

"Hi, Tata," she said. He tore a loaf of black rye bread into large chunks with his thick, muscular hands, bit into one hungrily, and held out a chunk to Miriana. She took it reluctantly, knowing that she could not say no, but she broke off only a little piece of it. Her mama joined them at the table, bringing the salad with her. Miriana watched as her father heaped his plate and passed the bowl to her. She picked out a few leaves and peppers for her plate but didn't eat them right away. Her stomach was still knotted.

"Miriana, aren't you hungry?" Nothing escaped her mother.

Miriana shook her head. "No," she mumbled.

"Are you sick? Did something happen at school today?" her mother persisted.

"No," Miriana lied. *Please just leave me alone,* she thought. Her parents wouldn't understand anyway. Her father hadn't completed public school, and he didn't place a very high value on education. Her mother looked after any writing or recording that was necessary for the business, but even she had only the basics of schooling.

Miriana poked at the food on her plate. The room was quiet; smacking lips and the occasional clink of a fork or knife against a dish were the only sounds.

Suddenly, a muffled boom in the distance shook the house. Miriana jumped in her chair. She stared at her mother with wide, questioning eyes. Her father stopped chewing.

"German tanks." Her mother answered the unspoken question. "The front has been moving closer to Bela Palanka. Did you notice more German soldiers in town this week?"

Tata dug into his food again. He was always the first finished, despite the enormous quantities he consumed. His appetite was healthy from a long day of hard labour, lugging heavy sacks of rye flour or manipulating logs in the sawmill.

"Miriana," her mother spoke again, "we had a telegram from your Aunt Lily today."

"Teta Lily? We haven't seen her for about two years—not since her baby boy was born. What does it say?" Miriana folded her arms across her stomach. Her aunt was her mother's younger sister, and there were at least 10 years between them. In some ways, Teta Lily was more like a sister than an aunt to Miriana because of their closeness in age. Teta Lily was twenty-seven, twenty-eight? Not thirty yet, anyway.

"She is arriving on the train. Tomorrow. With Zoran. The telegram doesn't tell us much, of course, but I have a feeling there is something that she couldn't put into the message."

Fumbling with her ruddy, thick, calloused hands, Miriana's mother withdrew a paper that she had folded into a little square and tucked into her apron pocket for safekeeping. She unfolded the paper and read aloud, "Arriving with Zoran Saturday train from Belgrade."

Miriana watched her mother's head as she bent over the paper and noticed, for the first time, that her mother's hair was laced with grey. Her mother looked up from the paper, meeting Miriana's eyes. Her square, healthy face, tanned and lined from years of outdoor work, furrowed at the brow, and her lips pressed tightly together.

"What's the matter, Mama? Aren't you happy to have Teta Lily and Zoran come for a visit?"

"This is wartime. Relatives don't travel a whole day on the train for a visit. Lily and Zoran will be staying." She paused. "Something must have happened to the Lowenthal family." She sighed, refolded the paper into its square, and tucked it back into her pocket.

"Do you mean they will live with us, Mama?"

Her mother nodded, "There's no mention of Ivan ..."

"But ... where can we put them in this little house?" Miriana blurted. She made a mental tour of their home: two bedrooms, a kitchen, a sitting room, a basement—and an outhouse. "Where will we put two more people?"

Her mother was quiet for a moment. The booming of tanks and guns in the distance increased in tempo.

"Zoran and Lily will take your room."

"My room? But where will I sleep? Where will I study? Where will I keep my books and clothing? Where will I change?" Miriana asked, the words tumbling out. "I won't have any privacy!"

"It's not easy, sweetheart," her mother continued, almost as if she had anticipated all the questions. "But we have to help when and where we can in this war. You will share our bedroom at night. You can hang some of your clothing with ours, and the things in drawers can go in the chest of drawers in the sitting room."

Miriana slumped back in her chair. She loved Teta Lily, really she did—and Zoran, even though she had never met him before. But the idea of giving up her room, where she was able to be alone with her thoughts, concentrate on her homework (*like today ... ha!*), and dress and undress in privacy, that was going to take some adjustment.

And for how long? she wondered.

"Saturday? But that's tomorrow!" Miriana sputtered, straightening suddenly.

Her mother nodded. "After dinner, while you clean up, I will go to the gypsy camp to tell Shasula she is needed tomorrow for cleaning. We will have to do everything by noon."

Miriana slumped back into her chair and watched her mother and father eat.

Her father stopped chewing. His mouth bulged with food that escaped between his lips as he spoke.

"Miriana, eat!" he commanded.

With reluctance, Miriana broke off a corner of bread and gnawed at it. It was dry and unappealing. With her fork, she moved the salad around her plate, spreading it out to make it look like she had eaten some. She thought again about school. Today had not been a good day, and tomorrow was full of uncertainty.

CHAPTER 2

The First Move

EVEN ON SATURDAY MORNINGS, THE MARKOVICH FAMILY was up early. Miriana's father planned to work at the mill until noon, and the sun was just peeking through the window when Miriana heard her parents in the kitchen.

She stretched like a cat in her warm bed, her arms folded behind her head for a cushion. She felt good, so secure, in that place. She thought about the day ahead and remembered with a start that her aunt and cousin were arriving.

Part of her was excited, and the other part hedged at the thought of two newcomers to the house. Her room. Her bed. Suddenly the thought struck her that tonight she had to give it all up and move in with her parents.

Miriana had never lived anywhere else that she could remember. She had spent her entire life in this centuries-old bungalow of white stucco mottled with yellow and black, beneath its red-orange terra cotta roof. How different life must be for her aunt, Teta Lily, a graduated lawyer living in Belgrade, the capital of Serbia. Miriana was impressed that her mother's sister had graduated from university, married a dentist, travelled, and, finally, settled in a large city. In a way, she had always looked up to Teta Lily. Of course, she loved her parents, but Teta Lily she admired.

The delicious aroma of Turkish coffee drifted into her room, and Miriana felt her tummy rumble. She was hungry. With a final stretch, she threw aside the feather ticking and got out of bed. She pulled off her nightie and pulled on her smock, hastily buttoning the little panel at the front but ignoring the cuffs. She didn't bother to look in the mirror. She knew how her hair would look—bushy, frizzy, and projecting from her head in uneven bunches. It would take too long to brush it, so she ignored it. She yanked on her blue Serbian slippers that were constructed like socks with leather bottoms, and she shuffled into the kitchen.

"Good morning," she said, addressing each of her parents. Her father had started eating already. He just nodded and grunted, but when she walked by, he grabbed her and hugged her, squeezing the breath out of her.

"Tata!" she protested.

He let her go and continued eating.

"Eat quickly, sweetheart," her mother prodded her. "Shasula will be here at any minute, and we have to start cleaning and re-arranging."

Miriana was still eating her porridge when Shasula arrived. Shasula wore a bright yellow peasant blouse and skirt nipped tightly at the waist. The fabric flowed around her curvaceous body. Although Shasula wasn't any taller than Miriana, Miriana was struck by the differences between the two of them. Shasula's body was already full and round, and Shasula flaunted it with every move. Miriana was still undeveloped by comparison. She had only a hint of breasts and modest hips, and, in her smock, even the suggestion of puberty was hidden.

Then there was the hair. Shasula's head shone with a glossy mane of kinky, thick, tousled, raven-black hair that always looked as if it was intended to be just that way—however it was.

"Morning!" Shasula called out, at the same time as the door slammed behind her.

"Good morning, Shasula," Miriana whispered, not looking up from the table.

"So, what we gonna do today, Missus?" Shasula asked, her smooth, brown arms crossed on her bosom, her hips and skirt swinging rhythmically while her bare feet tapped the wooden floor.

"You can start in the sitting room, Shasula. We have to empty the top two drawers of the chest for Miriana. Wipe them with a damp cloth. Then when Miriana has emptied her bedroom, we'll clean that thoroughly."

"Okay. I'll get the bucket and the soap," Shasula replied, and padded out of the room, singing in her rich melodic voice.

Miriana removed the things from her dresser and arranged them in the chest in the sitting room. She took her one other dress, her coat, and her nightie and hung them on hooks in her parents' room. Her last job was positioning her treasured mirror and brush set on the buffet in the sitting room. The buffet, another piece from her Baba, was fine and delicate with nimble legs. The buffet and the kitchen table seemed mismatched for their size and stature, but the colour of the wood was almost the same. A white lace doily Baba had crocheted for Miriana when she was born covered the surface of the buffet, adding to its daintiness. On the wall behind the buffet hung three decorative plates with pictures of Sveti Stevan, the family's patron saint.

Miriana watched Shasula and her mother string a cord the length of her parents' bedroom and hang a blanket on it, dividing the room in two. One half of the tiny room would be for Miriana. When she stretched out her arms, she could touch both the blanket and the wall.

Hardly a room, she thought.

By lunchtime, the house was clean and smelled sweetly of the soft, homemade soap they also used for their personal cleanliness. Miriana's mother paid Shasula with eggs and flour, and Shasula left, carrying her "pay" in a small straw basket.

A creaking and rumbling noise drew Miriana's attention to the yard. When she opened the door, she saw her father, Nikola, chatting with an older man who stood grinning and nodding proudly beside a docile, white ox. The man had only three teeth that Miriana could see, and his mouth looked shrunken, hardly big enough to accommodate even those few remaining teeth. He seemed to smile not just with his thin lips but with his eyes too. Everything turned upwards.

Tata had hired the ox and cart to transport Teta Lily, Zoran and their luggage back to the house. The wooden wagon, crudely constructed by the farmer, was sturdy and rough, but it would easily accommodate three people and luggage. Tata took the ox's lead rope, and Miriana and her parents started out, moving slowly, keeping pace with the plodding ox.

The train station was busy. People milled about on the platform, some chatting, some eating. The air smelled of garlic, eggs and fuel. Around the corner from the station sign that read *Bela Palanka*, White Town, Miriana spied a man urinating against the side of the building. She blushed and averted her eyes. German soldiers in neat, pressed uniforms and polished boots carried rifles on leather slings over their shoulders and paced the platform at regular intervals. Their boots thudded heavily on the wooden platform. Through the window of the little station house, she saw more German soldiers sitting at tidy desks.

The train was late, hours late, as expected, but there was no alternative but to wait. When it finally came chugging into the station, the excitement in the crowd was visible, palpable. Voices rose in pitch; hands rose in the air, waving vigorously, and bodies pushed and strained to get close to the track. Even Miriana felt a little flutter in her tummy as the large beast ground to a jerky halt. The brakes gave one final squeal, and, for a moment, the train was almost lost in steam. White clouds rolled up and around the monster as it exhaled with a loud *puh-uh-ush-sh-sh*. Soldiers yelled and prodded, keeping the crowd at bay while the passengers half-stepped, half-jumped from the stairs of the train.

When Teta Lily appeared at the exit, carrying Zoran and her bag, Miriana recognized her immediately. A tall, broad, handsome woman with white skin and peach-coloured cheeks, Teta Lily would have drawn attention anywhere. She looked stunning in a clear, bright red suit with matching hat and shoes.

Miriana saw Teta Lily hesitate at the train's exit, her eyes searching. *She can't see us*, Miriana thought. *We're just part of the crowd.*

Miriana's mother waved her arms high, but so many people were waving, they were just one more pair of arms.

"Lily! Lily!" she called until Teta Lily smiled, showing her straight, strong, white teeth. Miriana knew her aunt had spotted them. She watched as Teta Lily accepted the help of a German soldier who took her bag and her hand as she clambered off the high step. She saw them hesitate for a moment as if they were conversing, and then Teta Lily turned into the crowd. Miriana's mother pushed her way through the crowd from one end and Teta Lily from the other. The two sisters embraced, kissing and crying, with Zoran, sucking his thumb, trapped between them. Miriana stood quietly, watching, and after a few seconds, Teta Lily turned and embraced her too.

"You! Miriana! How you have grown! Look at you. Such a pretty girl!" Teta Lily exclaimed. Her eyes travelled down and up Miriana's body and stopped at her face. Miriana blushed and pulled her aunt tightly to her. She felt weepy. She wanted to kiss Zoran too, but he shrieked, pushed her away, and threw both arms around his mother. Miriana felt hurt despite her aunt's explanations that Zoran was overtired from the long journey.

Finally, Teta Lily embraced Miriana's father who stood silently beaming a welcoming smile at her.

"Ah, Nikola," she said, stepping back and patting him on the shoulder.

"Lily, how much luggage do you have?" Nikola asked.

"Just one trunk, and this bag that I'm carrying," she replied.

They had to move to the baggage car to claim the small trunk. Zoran clung to his mother; she carried him the length of the platform, shifting him from hip to hip. In the noisy crowd and the warmth of the June day, it seemed to take a long time to produce the papers and take possession of the trunk. Miriana's father struggled with it, but he was a sturdy man, used to lifting heavy weights. With a little help from Miriana's mother, he managed to load the trunk on the ox cart. Miriana felt hot and sticky in her rough cotton smock, but beside her father, she looked cool. Tata glistened with sweat, and beads of saltwater ran down his cheeks and neck.

A soldier, bellowing into a bullhorn in German, moved closer and closer to them as he pushed his way through the crowd.

He's coming towards us, Miriana realized, and suddenly she felt uneasy. What could he want? Was it …? Yes, it was the same man who had helped Teta Lily down from the train. Ignoring the rest of them, he put down the bullhorn and started speaking directly to Teta Lily. Their conversation was brief.

Teta Lily turned to her sister, "Militsa, he's looking for someone who speaks German and Serbian—someone to translate. He knows I speak German. I thanked him when he helped me off the train."

"You'd better go. It wouldn't be wise to say no. Here, give me Zoran," her sister replied.

She reached out for Zoran, but he tightened his grip on his mother's neck. Teta Lily spoke soothingly to him and gently pried him loose. He slid into Miriana's mother's arms, and Teta Lily rushed off with the German soldier.

"Mama! Mama!" Zoran screamed, holding out his little arms and kicking his feet.

Miriana felt a sharp blow on her arm.

"*Ow-w-w-w!*" she wailed, looking angrily at Zoran. His brown leather shoes, heavy and solid, beat the air.

Zoran cried the entire time his mother was gone. Miriana's mother rocked him and hugged him, but he carried on without letting up.

Let him cry, Miriana thought. Her arm hurt, and right then she didn't feel good about having Zoran stay with them.

Twenty minutes later, Teta Lily returned. Zoran grabbed his mother's skirt, his face wet from the tears, mucus dribbling from his nose. Whenever Miriana looked his way, he turned away sharply with a squeal, burying his head in his mother's skirt. A slimy, wet patch appeared along the side of Teta Lily's suit.

"What did the soldiers want?" Miriana inquired.

"There was an old man with no papers. He didn't speak German, and they didn't speak Serbian. I had to translate. The same questions, over and over. 'Where are your papers?' 'What's your name?' 'What are you doing here?' The poor old *deda* was so confused. In the end, they took him away." She paused. "Militsa," she said to Miriana's mother, "the soldier took my name and asked where I was staying. They will be coming to ask me to translate again."

"You had to do it. If you refused to co-operate you would have caused trouble for all of us. Let's go home, Lily. You must be tired."

Teta Lily and Zoran rode in the ox cart. Teta Lily had wanted to walk after the long train ride, but Zoran would not let go of her, and she was too tired to carry him. They rode together in the cart. Miriana walked quietly alongside with Tata and Mama.

It was past their usual suppertime when they finally arrived home. Miriana's mother had prepared pork and salad and hot marinated peppers before they left, and the odour of garlic and olive oil greeted them at the door. Miriana was hungry. She realized with surprise that she hadn't thought about the embarrassing scolding at school all day. She helped her mother set out the dinner.

"What can I do?" Teta Lily offered.

Miriana's mother waved at her to sit down. "You have your hands full with Zoran. Sit down. Tell us what happened."

Teta Lily sighed. Hugging Zoran, who was squirming in her lap, she took a deep breath and blurted, "The soldiers. They came for Ivan. It was about one in the morning. It was terrible." Her gush of words was followed by a gush of tears.

"When?" Miriana's mother asked patiently, her hands still for a moment.

Miriana tiptoed around quietly, not wanting to interfere and straining to hear.

"Last week. It all happened so fast. He was taken prisoner, and I got a notice. We had to vacate the house. The Germans wanted it for their headquarters. Three days. That's all the time I had to pack and make travel arrangements. *Bozhe, bozhe,* oh god. You can't imagine."

"But why, Teta Lily? Why did they take Techa Ivan?" Miriana blurted.

"Oh, because he was in the militia. Everyone in the militia was taken prisoner. I don't even know where they sent him!" She started to cry again.

Miriana felt sorry for her aunt, and she felt guilty for not wanting Teta Lily to have her room, but she said nothing.

They ate supper quietly. Teta Lily talked about the hell of her last few days. There was so much she had had to leave behind. She sniffed into a hanky all through the meal.

Zoran refused to eat, and his mother had to cajole him into taking a few pieces of bread spread with pork fat and a sprinkling of salt. Miriana brought him a small, knitted pig that her mother had made for her when she was little. It was soft and cuddly, Miriana's favourite toy. She offered it to Zoran. He took it, then, with a whine, heaved it onto the floor. Hurt by his reaction, Miriana picked up the pig, dusted it off, and put it under her arm.

Zoran took his thumb out of his mouth and screamed, "Me. Give me."

Miriana held out the pig for him. He took it and hurled it across the room again. When Miriana picked it up, he screamed. She felt hurt and confused.

"Nikola, bring the rocking chair for Lily," Miriana's mother said crisply. He grunted, and with no words, but with a shy smile, he got up from the table and left for the parlour, still chewing his last mouthful of food.

Teta Lily ensconced herself in the chair with Zoran in her lap. *Thu-thud, Thu-thud.* She rocked Zoran in the heavy wooden chair. Soon his eyelids drooped closed, fluttered, and closed again. Except for the distant boom of artillery, the house was quiet. Teta Lily looked as if she was almost asleep herself.

She looks peaked and pale, Miriana thought.

"Where can I put him to sleep?" Teta Lily asked.

Miriana opened the door to her room. "Here, Teta Lily. You can sleep on the bed, and Zoran will sleep rolled in blankets on a kilim on the floor for now."

"Go to bed yourself, Lily," Miriana's mother added. "You must be tired too."

"No, I'll help you tidy up," Teta Lily protested.

"No, Teta Lily. I'll help Mama," Miriana insisted.

Teta Lily put Zoran on the carpet and covered him tenderly with a blanket. "Good night," she said, hugging and kissing her sister and Miriana. "And thank you."

Miriana helped her mother tidy the kitchen in silence. It had been a long and stressful two days for her. She would have just liked to go to her room and close the door to be alone, to think and rest. But, of course, she couldn't. Tonight, she, too, would sleep curled in blankets on a kilim on the floor.

She was so unsure of her feelings. She wished she could talk to Stefan. She sighed.

Tomorrow, she thought.

CHAPTER 3

The First Day

WHEN MIRIANA WOKE IN THE MORNING, HER BODY ACHED. It had been a difficult night. The wooden floor had not been comfortable for her bony body, and she had tossed and turned. The loud, nasal snoring of her father had woken her several times.

Still, it was a bright, warm day again, and already the sun was hot.

I must have slept in, she thought. Her father would be up, she was sure of that.

When her thoughts turned to Teta Lily and Zoran, her heart skipped a beat. What was in store for her today, she wondered. She shuddered at the memory of Zoran's behaviour. Not for the first time, she felt a pang of pity for her aunt.

She heard voices. Her mother and … and Zoran! Such a happy, cheerful voice. Miriana was surprised. She rolled out of the blankets and pushed them to one side with her foot.

Later, she thought. *I'll fold them later.* She was too groggy to do it yet, and, besides, the happy voice in the kitchen intrigued her.

She opened the door quietly and, standing in the doorway, peered into the kitchen. Zoran sat at the table, stuffing his red, round, little face with bread. Between bites, he sucked the jam off his pudgy fingers and licked the drips that curled their way around the smooth crust. Mama was busy setting out clean dishes, washing the dirty ones and pouring boiling water into a teapot.

"What that?" Zoran asked, pointing at the brown pot, a crust of bread spilling from his open mouth. He shoved it back in.

"Camomile tea. It's for your mama," Miriana's mother answered, without even looking up.

"Where Mama?" Zoran persisted with his questions. Miriana guessed that there had been a string of them.

"Good morning, Mama. Hi, Zoran," she said, stepping into the room. Her stomach was growling, and Zoran's sticky bread looked appetizing. "Where is Teta Lily?"

"She's outside in the outhouse. She's sick. I'm just making her some chamomile tea to soothe her tummy. Are you hungry, Miriana? Have some bread and jam or honey. It's on the table. Help yourself. Would you like some coffee or milk?" Her mother's pace, like her voice, was constant. She never seemed to stop working.

"What's wrong with Teta Lily? Is it serious?"

"No, she'll be fine. Why don't you tell her the tea is ready and ask her to come in?"

"I'm here, Militsa." The door squeaked as Teta Lily entered the house. "Good morning, Miriana," she said softly. She brushed her lips against Miriana's tousled hair. Teta Lily's face was pale, and she smelled like vomit. She eased herself into the chair next to Zoran and caressed his cheek with the back of her hand.

Zoran grinned at her and ran his tongue in a circle around his shiny lips.

"*Mmm-mmm-mmm*, GOOD!" he exploded, and the crumbs and spittle formed a little cloud around his mouth and settled on his mother's upturned face. Teta Lily hardly seemed to notice. She wiped her face with Zoran's napkin and remained seated listlessly in her chair.

"Here, Lily; you need some tea. It will settle your stomach," Miriana's practical mama insisted as she poured the yellow-green liquid, splashing and steaming, into a cracked porcelain cup.

"*Hvala*, Militsa, thanks." Teta Lily put up her hand to try to stop her sister's generous gush of tea but to no avail. The cup stood full and steaming.

The smell of food titillated Miriana's hunger pangs. She spread some jam onto a thick slice of bread and bit into it with appetite. Her aunt sipped at her tea and nibbled on some dry bread at her sister's insistence. For a few moments, no one spoke. Miriana could hear only the smack of lips, the sip of tea, and the swoosh of water as her mother continued washing up.

Suddenly Zoran turned to his mother and grabbed her around the neck, clutching her with round arms. At the same instance, Teta Lily jumped up from her chair, desperately prying herself from his grasp, and lunged for the door.

Miriana sat rigid in her chair as she listened to her aunt heaving and retching over the edge of the little porch. She didn't have time to reach the outdoor toilet. Zoran burst into a loud wail as he climbed off his seat in a hurry and ran towards the door after his mother. The tablecloth stuck to his sticky hand and flipped the pot of jam onto the floor with a crash. Miriana's mother grabbed Zoran, and Miriana grabbed the cloth.

"Mama, Mama!" Zoran screamed, his arms and legs flailing. Gently his aunt Militsa pressed him against her body. After a moment, he stopped kicking and collapsed in a limp heap against her body, sobbing.

Miriana picked up the jam pot. The sticky vessel clung to her hand, and she took it to the basin to wash it off. Her mind was whirling.

What is this sickness Teta Lily has? Will we get it? Will Teta Lily get better? she wondered. And Zoran. She couldn't decide what she felt about him. One minute he was cute and cuddly and the next, a screaming, thrashing beast.

Mama wiped Zoran's face and hands with a damp cloth. As she stroked him gently, she cooed softly until he seemed pacified.

Miriana wiped the floor. She had lost her appetite and decided to go to the bedroom to dress. It wasn't such an easy task. Her dress was there on the hook, but her brush and comb were still in the sitting room. She had no room to move, so she folded the blankets, stacked them in the corner, and pulled her dress over her head. Still buttoning her worn frock, she went back into the kitchen.

Zoran, dressed in his short pants, sat playing with the toy she had given him last night.

He smiled and held up the pig. "Look, Yanna! My pig wants to get dressed too."

Miriana smiled back.

"Sertse, sweetheart, Teta Lily has gone to lie down. Mr. Goran just arrived with a log, and I have to help your father at the mill. Tata's waiting for me. Please, you have to look after Zoran. Take him outside so that his mother can get some rest." Her mother's voice was pleading with Miriana.

"Outside! We goin' outside?" Zoran slid off his chair and tugged at Miriana. "We gonna see pets?"

Miriana knew her mother was counting on her, and she couldn't disappoint her.

"Okay, Zoran. Let me brush my hair first, and then we'll go meet them all."

Her mother smiled faintly and was gone.

Miriana had lived with barnyard animals all her life. Each one was a pet, and she loved them all. Any time one of the animals was slaughtered for eating, her mother had to remind her that the animal's biggest pleasure in life was to be eaten. It worked, more or less, but Miriana still had reservations.

For Zoran, the presence of animals was a new excitement in life. He scurried among the chickens, cackling and strutting as if he were one of them.

"C'mon, chickie, have some corns," he coaxed. In his pudgy, half-closed fist, he held out a potpourri of grains. As he ran towards the nervous birds, they half-flew, half-ran away in various directions. Just when Zoran seemed close enough to feed one, the glassy-eyed bird would lurch and scramble away.

Miriana grinned as she watched Zoran toddling around the yard. She didn't worry about the chickens. She was confident they would protect themselves.

"Let me get you some more grain, Zoran," she called to him. She picked up the empty bucket and headed to the mill. She scooped up some loose grain from the floor and, swinging the pail, danced back to the barnyard. When she returned, she saw that Zoran had abandoned the chickens and was approaching the tall, white goose and her fuzzy goslings at the end of the barnyard.

Bozhe! Oh god, no! The chickens might flee from him, but the goose would not.

Stretching her tall, proud, neck, the pugnacious goose charged at Zoran. She honked and hissed, her broad orange-yellow beak open in a threatening V-shape, her wings spread at her sides like two giant sails, turning her body into a frightening size.

Zoran blanched. The bird was as tall as he was; as the goose craned her long neck towards his face, their eyes locked on the same level. Zoran seemed frozen in his tracks. Miriana dropped the pail and ran to him. She scooped up his still, little body in her arms, holding him above the level of the hissing goose until the bird dropped her wings and waddled off to be with her babies.

Miriana hugged Zoran until he relaxed in her arms.

How well I remember when this happened to me, Miriana thought. *I must have been just about the same age as Zoran. I was terrified!*

She looked at Zoran. His wide eyes were fixed on her. She gave him a squeeze and put him carefully back onto his feet. Hand in hand, they walked over to retrieve the spilled grain. She liked the feel of his tiny, warm hand in hers.

Teta Lily slept several hours that Sunday, and, by suppertime, she was feeling better. She was even delighted by the idea of walking into town to walk the corso, a social promenade that took place every evening after dinner. Homes were usually too small for entertaining. It was an old custom in Serbia for townsfolk to meet on the street to visit. That evening the flow of people was so strong that Miriana found it difficult to move in any other direction than the stream in which she was caught. No one knew as they paraded up and down the street that this would be the last corso until after the war.

Miriana hoped she would see Stefan. He didn't even know yet about the arrival of Teta Lily and Zoran. But she was disappointed; Stefan was not there. Probably he was home practising the violin. He liked the peace and quiet of that hour when his parents and grandparents were out.

As they arrived home, Miriana noticed a military truck parked in the yard. Two German soldiers waited at the house, one dark and the other fair. Both were tall, striking men. Miriana saw her parents exchange glances, but neither one spoke. Teta Lily stopped mid-sentence.

"I recognize those men," she whispered.

The soldiers clicked their heels and gave a slight bow as her aunt approached. They spoke to her in German in polite voices, and when they finished, Teta Lily turned to her sister.

"They want me to go with them to translate," she said. "Right now. Militsa, I'm afraid to go, and I'm afraid not to go."

"Go, go," Miriana's mother replied, waving her away with her arms. "Best not to rock the boat. I will put Zoran to bed."

Teta Lily turned to leave in the truck with the soldiers. When Zoran realized his mother was going, his sunny face turned stormy. He stood at the screen door and shrieked, "Mama, Mama."

When his mother didn't return, the tears brimmed in his eyes and rolled down his dusty cheeks, making lines where they crawled. Miriana's mother tried to coax him to put on his pyjamas and have some warm milk, but he just pushed her away with his arms.

"No, no," was all he would say, and he refused to budge from the door

Miriana wanted to help her mother, but she felt helpless.

What can we do, Miriana wondered. *What distracted me when I was his age?*

"Zoran," she called. Zoran continued to cry. "Let's go see if the chickens are sleeping. It's their bedtime, and they should be in their nests."

Zoran still cried.

"And Pasha the pig too, Zoran. Do you think he's in bed?"

Miriana knelt beside him. Zoran stopped crying and looked at her. The runny mucus made a continuous line from his nose to his mouth. He sniffed.

Yuck, thought Miriana. She felt like abandoning the plan, but her mother came with a damp cloth and wiped Zoran's face. When he was clean and fresh, Miriana squeezed his soft-skinned little hand in hers, and the two of them pushed together through the screen door, letting it clatter shut behind them.

It wasn't long before Zoran stopped sniffing and started chattering quietly and rubbing his eyes.

He's tired, Miriana thought, *but he won't give in just yet.*

Back in the house, Zoran took the hot milk his aunt had prepared for him, but he refused to put on his pyjamas.

Miriana, herself, felt tired and she couldn't understand Zoran's resistance to going to bed. When Teta Lily finally returned almost two hours later, Miriana went to prepare her things for school the next day and make her bed of blankets on the floor. She would get ready for bed, even if Zoran wouldn't. She closed the door tightly so that no one would see her undress. She felt self-conscious these days, and the changes to her body made her feel awkward. Her body was still thin and wiry, but her dresses were becoming tight as her breasts grew. There was the hair too. Nervously, she slipped out of her dress, took her nightie from the hook, and hung up her dress on the hook where the nightie had been. As she stood naked, the door flew open, and Zoran charged in, holding up his pyjamas.

"Look, Yanna! My 'jamas." The door stood wide open.

Miriana clutched the nightie to her naked body, her cheeks flushed. Teta Lily sailed in behind Zoran, swept him into her arms, and carried him out without a word, closing the door firmly behind her. Hastily, Miriana pushed her arms and head into the nightie. She couldn't get it on fast enough. The nightie was twisted, and she yanked at it in frustration until, at last, with a rip, it fell and covered her body.

She didn't even look to see where the rip had occurred. She rolled herself, exhausted, in the top blanket and lay there feeling her heart thud. As the beating slowed, she felt one tear escape, then another.

What's happening, she thought. *Everything's changing.*

Oh god, tomorrow's Monday, and I have that test, she suddenly remembered. *I'm not ready for it.*

Miriana lay in her makeshift bed, staring at the naked light bulb in the ceiling, and the thick, dark cord carrying the wires from the switch to the light. Her eyes blurred, and she let the tears trickle until she fell asleep.

CHAPTER 4

New Complications

SOMETIME IN THE NIGHT, MIRIANA WOKE UP. SHE FELT disoriented. Where was she? What time was it? What was that noise? It was still dark, and she could see the stars and the moon shimmering through the open window.

It's still night, she thought, *and this floor is uncomfortable. Oh, I hope Tata gets me a new bed soon.*

She heard the sound again. She listened carefully. The springs in her parents' bed were squeaking in a slow, rhythmic pattern. The sheets rustled, and she heard the whisper of her father's deep voice.

"Shh, shh!" It was her mother's voice. "You'll wake Miriana," she whispered.

Bozhe! Oh my god! They're doing it, Miriana realized. *They're ... having sex. I didn't think they did that anymore!* She lay rigid in her bed hardly daring to breathe as she listened to the sounds. An image of her parents naked, in bed together, flashed in her mind. She shut her eyes, trying to get rid of the picture, but it wouldn't go away. The sounds were still there too. Her father's breathing, her mother's soft, stifled laugh.

Carefully, so she wouldn't make any noise herself, Miriana wrapped the pillow around her ears to muffle the sounds. She lay, unmoving, until even through the puffy pillow, she could hear her father's shallow snoring.

She relaxed, let go of the pillow, and rolled over in the blankets, pulling them tightly around her. Exhaustion finally overtook her, and she felt herself drift off into sleep.

Monday morning, Miriana was late rising, and she had to rush to be at school on time. Zoran was already up eating breakfast. When she was ready to leave, he threw his arms around her neck and gave her a big hug and kiss.

"Miriana, go ask Shasula to come and help today. Lily is sick again," her mother said.

"But, Mama, I'm in a hurry," Miriana protested, glancing nervously at the clock and avoiding looking at her mother. She felt somehow embarrassed at being a witness to last night's activity. It was not something she could talk about.

"Sertse, sweetheart, either that or you stay home from school and look after Zoran and do the housework." Her mother was soft-spoken but firm. Miriana knew when she was defeated.

"Okay, Mama, I'm going." She gathered her few things and bounded out the door without kissing her mother.

The day went well for her, even though it seemed to be off to a slow start. The test was not as difficult as she had worried that it might be, and Mr. Josich, the teacher, gave no indication that he was still upset with her after the Friday incident. It was as if the note from Stefan saying, "Don't tell him anything!" had never been passed, and the teacher had not yelled at them. It all had started because Mr. Josich had been asking questions about home life, political affiliations, and parents' behaviour lately.

Why would he want to know all that? Miriana wondered.

Miriana's head was so full of thoughts about home that she was relieved when the school day was over and she had some time to be with Stefan. Stefan lived past her house, so if he was not going for his violin lesson, he usually walked home with her. They ambled along in the warm sun, silently at first. Miriana noticed that he was becoming brown from his work outdoors on his grandparents' farm. His hair looked the same whether he had just combed it or whether he had been sweating from doing chores. A mass of shiny dark brown curls tumbled over his forehead, sometimes covering his eyebrows. He stared at the ground intensely with large green-brown eyes framed by short, curly eyelashes. The cleft in his chin was deep and seemed to be more pronounced each year, and his muscles were harder and firmer from physical labour. As his grandfather aged, Stefan took over more and more of the work.

"I missed you at the corso on the weekend. My aunt is here, Teta Lily. And Zoran. He's two," Miriana began gingerly, not knowing where the words were going to take her next. "They came on the train on Saturday. To stay. I had to give up my room."

Stefan said nothing. He just glanced at her. She knew he was listening so she plowed ahead. As they walked along the dusty dirt road, she gave him an account of everything that had happened on the weekend—everything except the incident with her parents at night. She blushed again at the thought.

"And then, this morning, Mama wanted me to stay home from school." Miriana realized suddenly that she had been doing all the talking.

Stefan stopped, kicked at a clod of dirt in the road.

"But why?" he asked. Stefan's eyes met hers and then shifted wildly from her left eye to her right and back again, making her feel dizzy.

She was startled by the intensity of his gaze. "Well, Teta Lily was sick again, and Mama had to work at the mill with Tata," she explained. "But she sent me to get Shasula before she let me go to school. That's why I was so late."

Stefan dropped his eyes and started walking again.

"Why? What's wrong, Stefan?"

"That's how it starts," he said. "First you have to help out, then you have to miss the occasional day of school to work. Next thing you know, they want you to quit so that you can be there all the time."

"I don't understand. Did something happen?" Miriana asked.

"Oh, it's my mother. She wants me to quit school—and the violin. Stay home and work in the fields. You know I don't want to be a farmer. I want to play the violin. I want to go back to Belgrade to study. After this war, of course. It's bad enough that my hands are so coarse and calloused from all the work on the farm. It makes it difficult to *feel* the violin. I mean, I can put up with that as long as I know that there will be an end to it." He sighed. "But I don't see an end.

"And there's the cost. My mother says we can't afford it anymore. I work hard on the farm. Couldn't I have just this one thing?" He frowned. "I can't ask Chika Rajkovich to teach me for nothing. He's old and poor." He shook his head and walked faster.

Miriana was puzzled. Would his mother really do that? Did Stefan really believe her parents were thinking about keeping her out of school just because of this morning?

When they reached the house, she invited Stefan to come inside to meet her aunt and Zoran. She was not surprised when he refused.

"Gotta go. Got chores to do. Thanks anyway," he said. "Another time."

There was also violin practice after chores, she knew. And even though he wouldn't say it, he was too shy.

Stefan opened the gate for her but didn't come in himself. "Bye, Miriana. See you tomorrow," he said, closing the gate.

"Wait!" she said. "What did you mean 'Don't tell him anything' in that note on Friday? Mr. Josich sure was upset."

"He passes on what he finds out to the Nazis. He is just fishing for information that the Germans can use. He's kind of a spy. Lie if you have to, but don't tell him anything."

"How do you know all this?" Miriana queried.

"Chika Rajkovich. He's a smart old man. He's lived through war before."

"Oh," was all she could say as Stefan strode off.

Teta Lily was in the kitchen, preparing dinner. Shasula had gone, and Miriana's parents were still working at the mill. Teta Lily gave her a cheerful smile. She wiped her hands on a towel and hugged and kissed Miriana.

"How was your day?" she asked cheerily.

"It was fine, Teta Lily," Miriana answered. "But how are you? Mama said you were sick again this morning."

Her aunt sighed. "I'm fine, Sertse. But I think you and I should have a talk. Sit down, sweetheart."

Miriana felt her stomach knot. *Why do I feel this way?* she thought. *This is my favourite aunt talking.*

"First this, Miriana," Teta Lily said, holding in her hands the mirror that had been her grandmother's. Teta Lily handed it to her. The glass was shattered and several pieces of it were missing. "Oh, Miriana, I remember that this mirror is your favourite piece that Baba gave to you. I feel terrible about this. Zoran found it in the sitting room this morning. He was playing with it, and it broke. I'm sorry. All I can do now is promise to have it fixed. One day. I can't even say when. With the war, it may take a while. Please try to understand; Zoran's only two." She hesitated.

Miriana stared at the broken glass. She wanted to scream and shake her fists. Instead, she clenched the metal casing of the broken mirror tightly in her lap and said nothing.

"There's something else too, Sertse. I'm not really sick. That is, it's not a disease. What I have is called morning sickness. Oh, this is sounding so muddled. Miriana, I'm pregnant. I'm going to have a baby." Teta Lily stopped talking.

Miriana looked at her aunt. Of course! That explained the unusual nature of her aunt's sickness. But what did that mean? Another person in this already overcrowded house? More broken things? More temper tantrums? She felt hurt and confused. Not knowing how to respond, she let the mirror fall with a clatter on the table and stood up.

"I'm going to see if Tata and Mama need some help at the mill," she muttered and ran out the door, the telltale screen door giving its usual clatter and thump.

She didn't go to the mill. Instead, she followed the rivulet upstream into a small grove of oak and plum trees. She sat on the bank, hugging her knees to her chest; listening to the rippling of water, her mind sorted through the confusion.

One day at a time, she thought. *I'll just have to deal with each day as it comes.*

CHAPTER 5

A New Guest
November 1942

THE NOVEMBER LAND WAS COLD AND BARREN. HERE AND there, a grey, dry stalk, frosted with white, protruded from the naked fields. Chimneys puffed away, only at the coldest times, with delicate columns of smoke that made the air in the villages acrid. Guns boomed, sometimes near, sometimes far.

In the second trimester of pregnancy, Teta Lily recovered from morning sickness, and the family came to count on her to look after meals and housework. Miriana was content to go to school every day. In fact, Teta Lily insisted on it. Miriana found Teta Lily to be more knowledgeable and sophisticated than anyone she had ever met in Bela Palanka. She whetted Miriana's appetite for university and travel. After the war, of course.

"Miriana," she would say, "you are bright and capable, and you love learning. This war can't last forever. And when it does finally end, you have to come to Belgrade to study. Ivan and I will help you all we can." The name "Ivan" often triggered a sigh or a few tears from her aunt.

In the evenings, Teta Lily taught Miriana to speak German, and Miriana found that she had a real ear for the language. Zoran was learning too, and sometimes his pronunciation made her laugh. She looked forward to those times.

Early in November, Miriana came home from school to find Aleksandar Teshki sitting talking with her parents and Teta Lily. They were speaking in hushed voices. It wasn't usual for her parents to take time away from work during daylight hours.

Something must be happening, she thought.

As soon as she came in, they stopped talking. She expected her father to get up and give her a big bear hug, but he didn't. Even Teta Lily, who always embraced her, sat heavily in her chair, her swollen belly weighing her down. Zoran, who was playing on the floor, was the only one to greet her affectionately. He ran to her, threw his arms around her middle, and held on tight. Miriana picked him up and hugged him in return.

"Hello, Mr. Teshki," she said, uncomfortable with the sudden silence of the adults. Miriana never felt at ease with this man whom her parents called *Atsa*. Even when he came by for their *slava*, the annual celebration of the family's patron saint, she found it difficult to be anything more than civil to the man. She could serve him prosciutto and plum brandy at the parties, but she could never have a conversation with him. She noticed that her parents seemed to interact with him without a problem. In fact, she believed, they respected him.

"Miriana," said her mother, "please put Zoran's heavy blue sweater on him, and take him outside for a walk in the yard. We need to meet privately. Then we will be having dinner."

"Yes, Mama." Grasping Zoran by the hand, she led him into the bedroom and hunted for his sweater. She strained to hear what they were saying in the other room. She couldn't help being annoyed with Zoran. Every time he spoke, she missed part of the conversation.

"Caught … certain death for all of us." She heard Teta Lily's voice.

"Yanna, we gonna see Pasha?" Zoran asked. He tugged at her arm.

"Yes, Zoran. Shh, shh."

More voices from the living room.

"How long will it be for?" Mama speaking.

"Yanna, we gonna feed the chickens? You gots some corns or grains?"

Oh, Zoran, do be quiet, Miriana thought. "Yes, Zoran," she answered, in a whisper.

"Where can we … in the cellar? All day? Zoran might say … soldiers come to ask me to translate, regularly … get caught." Teta Lily again.

Miriana missed much of Atsa's next reply.

"Tonight, in a wagonload of corn … wait until dark … grind the corn as usual … Alex Bogdanovich will pick it up." Atsa's voice.

Miriana knew she had stalled as long as she could. She led Zoran out of the bedroom and through the kitchen to the back door. The adults had their heads bent in discussion and hardly seemed to notice them.

"Only till Christmas," was the last remark she heard.

She would just have to be patient, but the wait seemed interminable. When she saw Atsa Teshki leave, she knew she and Zoran could go back inside. They were red-faced and cold, but Zoran never seemed to be bored with the farm animals, no matter how long they spent with them.

At dinner, Zoran was the only one who said much at the table. Everyone else seemed to be engrossed in thought. Miriana wanted to ask so many questions, but she knew her mother would tell her when she wanted her to know. Besides, they probably wouldn't say anything revealing while Zoran was present.

While they were still at the table, a peasant pulled into the yard with a wagon loaded with corn. Miriana's father went out to talk to him. She could see them guide the ox pulling the load over to the mill, unhitch the animal from the wagon, and leave the load of corn sitting there. Zoran watched from the door. He wanted to go visit the ox, but his mother insisted he stay inside. He refused to eat any more supper and stood with his face pressed to the glass of the door until the man left with his beast and his uncle came back inside. He nodded to Militsa and sat down to finish eating.

This is the longest meal, Miriana thought. The words from her parents' conversation with Mr. Teshki and her aunt kept repeating in her head. She finished quickly and helped her mother tidy up while her father ate. Teta Lily took Zoran to get him ready for bed.

When Zoran was settled, the two women sat on the sofa, knitting. Miriana's father paced back and forth in the small room. Periodically, he would stand with his hand on the knob of the door that led to the backyard, then abruptly turn and begin pacing again. Miriana sat at the table with her books and tried to do her assignments for school. A clock ticked quietly in the room, counting out the seconds.

By nine o'clock, the village was in darkness. All the windows were curtained, blocking the light of bulbs or candles from escaping to the outside and guiding potential aircraft to a target. Miriana's father dressed himself in his heavy coat, muttered to his wife, and went outside. Mama put down her knitting and got up. She went to the stove and put on a pan of soup to warm.

"Miriana, there is something you must know," she said. "But first, I have to turn off the lights. We can talk in the dark." She pulled at the chain and the house became black. "We are hiding a soldier—a Serbian Partisan—in the cellar. He will be here only until Atsa can find him a place in the hills to hide. Till Christmas, maybe. No one must know he is here. If the Germans find out that we are hiding him, they will execute us all."

"But Mama, what about Zoran? He's so little. How are we going to keep him from saying something, especially when the soldiers come for Teta Lily?"

Her mother sighed. "That's a risk, Sertse. We will all have to be careful, especially with Zoran, as you said. He is sure to find out about the soldier's presence unless we keep him away from the cellar. And whenever someone comes to the mill, we'll have to be extra careful. We have to keep Zoran from talking. You just can never be sure who you can trust these days."

The door opened with hardly a sound. Miriana recognized the stocky outline of her father even in the dark. The other man, the soldier they were hiding, she presumed, was tall and lanky. It was difficult for Miriana to distinguish any facial features in the dark, but she could determine that the man had dark hair and a rough-shaven face with no beard or moustache. And he smelled. It was a strange combination of body odour, dust and manure.

"This is Josif," her father said, in a low, gruff voice, and Miriana's mother introduced herself, Miriana and Lily. They used only first names.

Her father opened the cellar door. "Josif, over here," he growled.

The stranger followed him to the cellar stairs. A trail of cornhusks fell from his clothing as he walked.

He has been hiding in that wagonload of corn all this time, Miriana realized with a start. *Poor man,* she thought. *It's cold out there.*

Mama ladled hot soup into a large bowl. She broke off a chunk of dark bread, poured a glass of water, and assembled it on a tray.

"Here, Miriana," she said. "You take this down to Josif. I have to get him some bedding."

Miriana took the tray and gingerly made her way down the steep-pitched wooden stairs. Her father had curtained off the cellar window, and a small, round naked bulb shed a dim light from the ceiling beam.

She set the tray of food carefully on a shelf. When she looked up, she gasped.

The soldier, standing in the lighted area, was not wearing a uniform. He was clad in a rough, brown shirt under a heavy, knitted, dark blue sweater and a pair of ripped black pants that were short in the leg revealing heavy, worn boots. In his hand, he clutched a black, knitted cap. His black hair stood in stiff peaks with dust interwoven and straw poking out. But it was his face that startled her. He looked about seventeen.

Why, he's barely older than Stefan. Or me, Miriana thought.

Josif met her gaze for a split second, but he quickly lowered his eyes. Feeling her cheeks flush, Miriana turned and bolted for the stairs. Her mother was coming down with two blankets and a pillow tucked under her arms. Josif would also sleep without a bed, rolled in blankets, but in the cold, damp cellar. She squeezed past her mother and ran up the stairs, her shoes clattering on the firm wood.

Teta Lily was putting away her knitting when Miriana arrived in the kitchen.

"What's he done, Teta Lily? Why does he have to hide?" Miriana blurted breathlessly.

"I don't know all the details," her aunt replied. "All I can tell you is that he was imprisoned by the Germans and somehow managed to escape. They will be looking for him, and if he is caught, he will be killed. You understand why we have to help him, don't you?"

Miriana hung her head and nodded. "Two months?" she whispered. "And would they really kill us all for hiding Josif?"

Her aunt nodded, her face grim.

This little house was bulging with tension. Miriana took a deep breath and exhaled slowly.

One day at a time, she reminded herself. *And we must be out of blankets by now.*

Chapter 6

A Close Call

Miriana took meals to Josif every day for the first three weeks after his arrival. Zoran still hadn't seen him. The family lived in fear that Zoran would learn of his presence and talk of him to others. They had worked out a plan so that Zoran was constantly diverted from the cellar. Josif's meals were taken down, and his basin for urine was removed only when Zoran was in the barn or at the mill. Miriana frequently took Josif his meals. She knew that the basin came and went, but she was never asked to help with it. She was silently grateful.

Josif only dared to go outside after dark and then only on the darkest of nights. Miriana heard her father giving him strict orders to remain absolutely quiet during the day, and he was co-operative.

Josif was shy, like Miriana, and, often, the meal transaction transpired without a word being spoken. The first time he said anything was a simple "Thank you" as he hung his head and seemed to concentrate on the dirt floor.

Miriana had blushed and found the words, "You're welcome," stuck in her throat. Each trip became a little less uncomfortable, and, as the days passed, she found she could smile and whisper, "Hello."

One chilly Saturday, as she passed the tray to him, she found herself looking into his eyes. They were a dark intense brown. At first, she saw sadness, but then they seemed to light up as his mouth curled into a faint grin. For the first time, Josif was real to her. She allowed herself to hold his gaze for a moment before his eyes flickered. Then she spun around and clattered up the steps. At the top of the stairs, she leaned against the closed door for a moment to catch her breath and her thoughts.

How would I feel if that were Stefan down there—every day, all day, day after day? she wondered. *How would I feel if that was me?* She shuddered.

Through the window, Miriana could see her aunt standing in the yard, her hands thrust into her pockets to protect herself against the cold, her coat straining against the buttons around her pregnant belly. Zoran darted back and forth in enthusiasm.

I must tell them it's safe to come inside, Miriana thought. Teta Lily will want to get to the market. Miriana had agreed to look after Zoran while her aunt did the shopping.

"Zoran, come in," she called out. Teta Lily waved, and, after kissing Zoran, she left through the gate, her basket swinging on her arm.

"C'mon, little man, let's play jacks." Miriana pulled six pig knuckles her father had given her and a little bouncy ball from a box on the mantle. Zoran couldn't really manage to scoop up the knuckles or catch the ball, but he chased the ball all over the room, squealing when she bounced it as high as she could for him. When he tired of the game, he curled up on his bed with a blanket and a picture book.

Miriana picked up the knitting she was preparing for Christmas. Her fingers flew up and down, forward and back, with the wool, and the needles clicked, *ONE-two, ONE-two,* as she pushed and pulled the yarn over and through. Outside, the mill whirred, and inside, wood crackled in the stove. Now and then, she heard a creaking noise come from the basement.

In the distance, Miriana suddenly heard the purr of a motor. The purr became a roar. She recognized the sound: it was a German military truck. She put down her knitting and listened.

Please let it go on by, she prayed, but the truck lurched to a stop at their gate. Brakes squealed; a door slammed. *Oh god, not now*, Miriana thought. She got up and looked out the window. It was a German soldier all right. And he was coming to the house.

"Who that, Yanna?" Zoran asked, looking up from his book.

"Just a soldier, Zoran. He probably wants your mama to translate," she answered, still staring out the window. Her mind raced. *What about Zoran? Josif? Bozhe, bozhe, oh god.*

The soldier knocked at the door, and without waiting for an answer, he barged inside.

"I'm looking for Mrs. Lowenthal. Is she here?" he bellowed in German. He was blond with ruddy cheeks, high cheekbones, soft blue eyes and straight white teeth. Miriana recognized him. He had come before. *What was his name? Hans? Yes, that was it.*

He is good-looking, Miriana thought, in spite of her nervousness. She remembered that the last time he had come he had been with another soldier, Kurt. Shasula had been here, and she had been flirting with the two men.

Where is Kurt now? she wondered. They usually travelled in pairs.

"I'm looking for Mrs. Lowenthal. Is she here?" he repeated in German.

Miriana understood what he wanted, but her tongue felt like a block of wood. She struggled to answer.

"*Nein. Sie ist im Dorf,*" was the best she could do, not sure if she had it correct or even if he was going to understand that Teta Lily was in town.

He replied quickly, and she didn't understand.

She shook her head. "*Nicht verstehen,*" she whispered. "Don't understand."

The soldier took off his coat and repeated the words, slowly, and this time Miriana understood that he would wait. She offered him a chair by the stove.

"*Danke,*" he said, smiling at her, "Thank you." His blue eyes flickered, and she watched them as they travelled down her body and up again. She felt her face burn, and she stood rooted to the floor. Part of her liked this young man, and the other part was afraid of him.

Zoran grabbed her legs. He had been so quiet for a moment that she had forgotten he was there. She put her hand on his curly hair.

"Zoran, go look at your book. Your mama will be home soon. The soldier is waiting for her to translate, that's all." Still he clung to her, his eyes fixed on the soldier.

Hans reached into his pocket and pulled out a flat bar. "*Schokolade?*" he asked. He held out a chocolate bar to Zoran. Zoran's eyes grew large and round. He looked at Miriana and then back at Hans.

"Go ahead, Zoran. You can have it," she said.

Zoran took the chocolate bar to his corner, and he unwrapped it with care.

I think that's the first one he's had since he has been here in Bela Palanka, Miriana thought.

"*Fraulein, bitte machen Sie mir einen Kaffee,*" Hans said, looking at Miriana and miming drinking. She understood "coffee" and nodded her head. She filled the *dzesva,* the Turkish coffee pot, with water and put it on the stove. While she waited for the water to come to a boil, she picked up her knitting. It was quiet again. She could hear Zoran smacking his lips and sucking his fingers. She was conscious of every little noise.

There was a gentle knock from the cellar. Miriana jumped

nervously. She glanced at Hans, but he didn't seem to have noticed. Her hands trembled, and she kept dropping stitches.

The coffee! Miriana was so nervous she had forgotten to grind the beans. She dropped her knitting into a bag, sprang up and rushed to the cupboard. The coffee mill was on a high shelf, and she had to stretch to reach it. She stood on her toes and supported herself on the counter with one hand while she groped for the square, wooden machine with the large crank. She felt it, grabbed it, and pulled it from the ledge. Her body recoiled like a spring as she whipped around, coffee mill in her hand.

The room blurred. She saw only green-brown, the colour of evergreens, the colour of Hans's uniform. She felt the prickle of rough fabric and heard the snap of buttons as she brushed against him. She gasped and inhaled. She detected the combined scent of damp wool and metallic cologne. She was caught between the counter and Hans's body.

She tilted her chin, and her eyes locked with Hans's. Her heart beat wildly, and she was shaking. She felt a rush of blood to her face and knew she must be blushing.

Hans spoke to her. Miriana wanted to understand, but it was hard to concentrate.

"*Hilfe?*" She grasped the word "help."

He is asking if he can help, she thought. She shook her head. "*Nein, danke,*" she whispered. "No thanks."

Hans stepped back a pace. He gave a curt nod and strode over to the window. He turned his back on the room, standing "at ease" with his hands clasped behind his back, and he gazed out the window.

Miriana found there was enough ground coffee left from breakfast. She didn't have to grind any more. Her hands shaking, she poured teaspoons of sugar and coffee into the Turkish coffee pot, spilling sugar on the hot stove. The granules ignited into miniature sparks that snapped and crackled, smelled of burnt caramel and then settled as soot on the surface of the stove. She let the coffee boil up three times in the brass pot and then put then put it aside to settle. Its delicious aroma filled the room.

When it was ready, she poured a cup for the soldier. He was still standing at the window.

"*Kaffee, mein Herr?*" she called softly.

Hans turned and looked directly into her eyes. Miriana felt herself blush again. His eyes fell to the cup of steaming coffee she was holding in her hand. The cup rattled in the saucer, and a dribble of *kaymak*, the milky foam that formed on the surface of the coffee, trickled down the side of the cup. Hans rushed over to Miriana and, without a word, took the coffee and sat down at the table to drink it.

"Me too, Yanna. I want coffee." Zoran hopped from his corner and sat down at the table with the soldier. Hans grinned. Miriana took Zoran's cup from the cupboard, filled it with milk and poured a splash of coffee on top to make it brown.

"*Mmm, mmm,*" Zoran slurped the coffee, his eyes on Hans. He matched Hans sip for sip. When Hans rested his cup on the saucer, Zoran put his down too.

Hans finished his coffee. "*Gut, danke,*" he said, nodding to Miriana. "Good, thank you."

Like an echo, Zoran piped up. "*Gut, danke,*" he said to Miriana and laughed.

Hans laughed with him. He stood up and wandered about the room, stopping every now and then to ponder some object in the room. Occasionally, he picked up an item and fingered it.

Miriana glanced at the clock. Teta Lily had been gone for more than an hour and a half. When would she return? Miriana was worried.

Hans stopped at the bedroom door and asked something.

She shrugged. "*Nicht verstehen.* I don't understand," she said.

The soldier pushed open the door to the bedroom and poked his head inside.

"*Ist das Ihr Schlafzimmer?*" he spoke to Miriana, but again, she didn't understand. "*Du?*" He simplified the question.

She understood "you," and she nodded.

"*Und Mutter und Vater?*" Miriana nodded again. Hans tilted his head and gave her a curious look.

"Mine room!" Zoran jumped up from his blanket and ran to his bedroom. "See," he said, proudly opening the door for Hans and inviting him inside.

The only door left now is the door to the cellar, Miriana thought. *My god, what am I going to do.* She put down her knitting and pushed into the bedroom past the soldier and Zoran.

"Zoran, why don't you take Hans out into the yard and show him the animals. Show him Pasha, the pig, and Pile, the chicken ... and ... and ... all the others. Here, let me help you put on your sweater."

"No, Yanna, I don't wanna go outside. Cold outside." He ignored her attempts to make him put his sweater on. She tried again, but he just shrugged it off.

"C'mon, Zoran, you can visit the mill and see what Uncle Nikola is doing." She shoved his arm into the sleeve of his sweater, and he yanked it out. Zoran darted for the bedroom door. Miriana followed. When she looked up, Hans was no longer in the bedroom.

"Zoran," she shouted. She really wanted to shout *Hans*. "Where are you?"

"Me gonna show Hans the cellar," Zoran replied. He was tugging on the doorknob with his two pudgy hands.

Hans said something to him in German and gently pried Zoran's hands from the knob. He took the handle in his strong, wiry fist, pulled, and with one yank, the door swung open.

"Hello! Hi, Zoran, it's Mama. I'm home!" It was Teta Lily's voice. She darted across the kitchen, swept Zoran up with one arm and closed the door to the cellar firmly with the other, her shopping basket still attached to her arm. "Zoran, you must not go down the steps alone. You could fall and hurt yourself. Mama told you many times."

Zoran hugged his mother and, with his nose pressed against hers, replied, "Hans take me."

Teta Lily spoke to Hans in German. He clicked his heels together and gave a short bow. "*Ja*, yes."

Miriana understood "yes," but she lost the rest of what was said. Hans put on his hat and coat.

Teta Lily turned to Miriana and handed her the shopping basket. "I saw a truck in the yard on my way home so I hurried the rest of the way. I told Hans we should go right now before I have to take off my coat and put it back on again. Will you take Zoran?"

Miriana nodded. She was still trembling.

Her aunt put Zoran on the floor. She gave Miriana a bear hug and whispered in her ear, "You're a brave girl. I love you."

Teta Lily left with the soldier, and Miriana was once again alone with Zoran—and the soldier in the cellar.

Zoran surprised Miriana. He didn't cry when his mother left. Before the truck engine roared, he ran to the cellar and starting tugging. "Yanna, you want to come too?"

Miriana wanted to collapse on her bed and cry until the tension drained itself from her body, but she didn't. Something inside her pushed her to respond to the crisis. She grabbed Zoran, holding him upside down. Zoran squealed, his hair flopping and brushing the floor. She swept him back and forth like a broom.

"I'm sweeping the floor with you, Zoran Lowenthal," she sang out.

Zoran laughed in high-pitched shrieks. His eyes were huge and round, his face red.

"And I'm not going to put you down until you promise to come and feed the poor, starving animals. Agreed?"

Zoran could hardly speak for laughing. "Okay, Yanna."

Gently, Miriana set him down on the floor. Before he could

change his mind, she found their sweaters. She carried both Zoran and the sweaters out under her arm and didn't stop to dress him until the front door was closed behind them.

That was too close for comfort, she thought. *Thank god, there are less than four weeks until Christmas. Josif should be safely gone by then.*

CHAPTER 7

Happy Christmas
January 6 and 7, 1943

CHRISTMAS WAS ALWAYS EXCITING FOR MIRIANA, AND THIS year was no exception even though her mother had explained in her quiet, affirmative way that there wasn't any money for gifts. It was almost impossible to find things to buy anyway, no matter what the cost. Miriana had lived long enough with austerity that she understood.

Josif had left the day before Christmas. Atsa Teshki made arrangements for him to join a band of Partisans in the hills, and he had been smuggled out the way he had come, in an ox cart.

Miriana was both relieved and sad to see him go. She admired his courage. They had become tentative friends, but the tension of his hiding in the cellar was sometimes unbearable.

Just before he left, Miriana presented him with a pair of socks she had knitted for him. She remembered how he had stuffed the socks into his pocket and grinned. "*Hvala*, thanks," he had said. His eyes sparkled, and she knew he was pleased.

Miriana had been busy preparing her few gifts in secret. There would be something for Mama and Tata, of course, and, this year, gifts for Teta Lily, Zoran and Stefan. Stefan had invited her to come for dinner on Christmas Day, and she had baked a loaf of bread for his mother. This was the first time she had been to his house for a meal, and she was both nervous and excited. She had washed and pressed her brown smock for the occasion. The dress wasn't pretty anymore, and it was too tight, especially across her bust, but it was the only one she had she could fit into.

Mama and Tata finished work early on *Badne Vece*, Christmas Eve. Teta Lily and Miriana had prepared the evening meal of unleavened bread, fish Tata caught in the stream, cooked beans, sauerkraut, and noodles with walnuts. A roast suckling pig, the traditional dish Christmas day, should have already been in the oven, filling the house with the mouth-watering aroma of cooked meat, but this year, there would be no pork. Zoran was too excited to eat. He swallowed a few mouthfuls when his mother insisted he couldn't open gifts without first eating some of the food. For him, the gifts were more special than dinner.

"Militsa, Nikola, we eat so well here. Thank you, thank you. Food is so scarce in the city. I can't tell you how much I appreciate your generosity in taking us in." Teta Lily's eyes were moist, but her smile told Miriana how happy she was. Militsa's response was to urge her to take more food.

"You finished, Yanna? You know what I made you for Christmas?" Zoran was up and down from the table, and he could hardly keep still.

"Teta Mi't'sa, we gonna light the tree, now?" At his aunt's nod, he turned to his uncle. "Techa Nik'la, c'mon."

Miriana's father belched and pushed his chair away from the table. He scooped Zoran up in his arms. "You light the first candle this year," he said. He shifted Zoran to his left arm, and, with his free hand, he took a long, lean piece of tinder that he lit in the wood-burning stove. "Here, Zoran," he said, cautiously holding the slender stick.

Zoran took the stick in his greasy hand. Nikola wrapped his burly fist around Zoran's hand and guided him in lighting the first candle on the tree.

Miriana watched with curiosity. It had always been she who lit the first candle, accompanied by warnings about the danger of fire with a flame around the evergreen tree. She looked at Zoran's cherubic face, red, scrubbed, and glowing in the light of the flame.

I'm glad Teta Lily and Zoran are here, she thought. She felt settled and more secure than she had at the start.

The first candle flamed. "Bravo, Zoran!" she yelled.

"Now, my little girl," Tata said. "Zoran, give the stick to Miriana."

"Tata," Miriana scolded, and she blushed. "I'm not little anymore."

Each of them took a turn lighting the candles until the tree was ablaze with flickering lights.

Zoran wiggled until his uncle let him down. He ran to the bedroom and returned with a box. In it, eight cookies were laid on a sheet of brown paper. With great care that surprised Miriana, Zoran extracted them, one by one, and handed them with pride to each one present. "It for you, Yanna. I make it."

"*Mmm, mmm,*" Miriana said, biting into her cookie. "It's delicious."

"Teta Mi't'sa, Techa Nik'la, Mama ..." Zoran continued. He held up each of the remaining cookies to account for them and then laid them back in the box. "For Shas'a, for Stefan. And Tata, when he comes back."

Miriana heard a sob escaped from Teta Lily. There were tears trickling down her face.

Poor Teta Lily, Miriana thought as she looked at her aunt closely for the first time in months. Teta Lily's hands were rough and calloused, and her body was swollen with the pregnancy. The clothing she wore to accommodate her growing belly made her appear more like a local peasant than an educated, sophisticated lawyer from the city. She had fashioned some loose garments from second-hand clothing she bought from a widowed farmer. In her plain, white blouse and long, black skirt, the traditional garb of rural women, she looked as if she really belonged in the countryside. Her hair was still beautiful, but she wore it pulled back and gathered into a tight bun at the nape of her neck; it looked severe against the soft lines of her face.

Zoran had one cookie left. He held it up and announced loudly, "For me!" He opened his mouth wide and crunched down on the tip of the crescent-shaped almond cookie.

Tata guffawed noisily and rumpled Zoran's hair. Teta Lily sputtered and laughed, even though the tears continued to roll down her face. Miriana felt her feelings turn upside down, and she joined her aunt's laughter. Zoran finished the last of his cookie and sat licking the remnants of powdered sugar from his fingers.

Quietly, Miriana slipped into the bedroom for her gifts. Nothing was wrapped.

"Tata, for you," she said, and handed him socks. Her father grunted his pleasure and planted a noisy kiss on her cheek.

Miriana blushed. "Teta Lily," she continued, "well, it's not really for you. It's for the baby." She handed her aunt a tiny, green sweater with a tie and tassels at the neck.

"Oh, Sertse," Teta Lily exclaimed as she held the sweater up to look at it carefully. "It's beautiful. You did such a fine job. Thank you, sweetheart. It's a perfect gift." She squeezed Miriana in her arms and held her tightly against her. Miriana felt a little bumping in her aunt's belly. "That's the baby kicking. It thanks you too!" said Teta Lily, smiling.

Zoran tugged at Miriana's sleeve. "What you got for me, Yanna?" he queried.

"This!" she replied, grinning. *"Oink, oink."* She held out a little stuffed pig similar to her own.

Zoran squealed. "Mine?" he asked. Miriana nodded. He grabbed the knitted pig, hugged it and made snorting noises.

"What are you going to call him, Zoran?" she asked, smiling from ear to ear. His enthusiasm for the gift made her feel so good.

"Hmm. I think I'm going to call him *Pasha*," he replied, crushing the pig in his arms.

"Mama, this is for you. I know it's not much." She handed her mother a knitted cover for the teapot.

"Miriana, you've been busy knitting. No wonder the wool supply is disappearing! Thank you, Sertse." Her mother put her arm around Miriana's neck and hugged her.

"My turn," said Teta Lily. From a high shelf, she produced a book for Zoran. She opened it to the middle and showed him the colourful pictures. "Even in wartime, we must read," she said. "Zoran, look. This book is about animals. Who's this?" she asked as Zoran climbed into her lap and became absorbed in the pictures. He still held his pig tightly under his arm, Miriana noticed with pleasure.

"And the last one is for you, Miriana," Teta Lily said, looking up from the book. "It's hanging behind the bedroom door. Can you get it, please?"

Miriana was surprised, and she hesitated for a second. She really didn't expect anything. And then she went to look behind the door. As she swung open the heavy, interior door, there was swish of red. She stopped and stared. It was a dress. And it looked like the red suit Teta Lily wore when she first arrived in Bela Palanka by train.

"I made it over for you," Teta Lily explained. "You need something that fits you, and it certainly doesn't fit me anymore." She laughed.

Miriana gaped at the beauty of the dress. She ran her hand over the smooth, finely textured fabric. She fingered the minuscule red buttons that closed the cuffs of the sleeves and the bodice. She lifted the hem and exposed the satiny lining under the skirt. Her lower lip trembled, and she bit on it to stop the shaking.

"Try it on. Let's see if it fits," her mother urged.

Miriana took the dress off the hanger as if it would fall apart if she fingered it too much; her hands shook. She took it into the bedroom, struggled out of her tight brown smock, and stepped into the new red one. One by one, she fastened the tiny buttons until they were all in place. It fit. She felt she could breathe easily. It didn't bind her body as the old brown one had. Looking down, she twisted her hips and watched with pleasure as the fabric swirled and wrapped itself around her body, stopped, and swung back in the other direction. The air was filled with a soft, floral scent of Teta Lily's cologne.

It's the most beautiful dress, she thought.

Shyly, she stepped out of the bedroom in her new dress and bare feet.

Her mother gasped. "*Ow-ww*, Miriana, you are so beautiful!" she said. Her father grunted approvingly, and Teta Lily beamed. Miriana rushed to her aunt and threw her arms around her. She didn't trust herself to speak because she knew she would burst into tears.

Oh, Happy Christmas, she thought. *War or no war.*

The next morning, Miriana was elated. It didn't matter that St. Nicholas hadn't had sweets to leave in her shoe that Christmas Eve. She had her gift, the most marvellous gift, and so unexpected. Of course, she would wear the new dress for Christmas dinner at Stefan's house. It felt so good when she put it on, so loose and comfortable, so soft and silky against her skin. She spent extra time in front of the mirror piling her hair on top of her head just like she had seen Teta Lily's hair in photographs. Her hair was no more co-operative that morning than it ever was, but Miriana exercised great patience in combing and fastening it with pins until every lock was secured against her head.

When Stefan arrived, she was the only one in the kitchen. Her mother and father were looking after the animals, and Teta Lily was in the bedroom dressing Zoran. Stefan knocked at the door with his cold fist and stood pounding snow off his boots while he waited for the door to open.

Miriana swung open the heavy, interior door and greeted him cheerily. "*Zdravo*, Stefan!"

He grabbed the storm door and yanked it open without even looking. When he saw Miriana, he stopped and stared. Both doors were wide open, and the cold air blasted the inside of the house, but Stefan stood rooted to the spot. Miriana felt the blood rush to her face. Her cheeks darkened to the shade of an overripe peach. Neither spoke.

Finally, Stefan stepped inside the kitchen and let the outer door slam shut. He fixed his eyes on the floor and stammered. "You … you … you look different," he blurted.

"It's cold in here! Close that door!" Teta Lily shouted from the bedroom. She came into the kitchen carrying Zoran. "Stefan, *Srechan Bozhich!*" She greeted him with three kisses on alternating cheeks.

"Same to you, Mrs. Lowenthal, Merry Christmas," he replied. He turned to Miriana. "Are you ready to go?"

She nodded and went to get her coat and hat. The socks for Stefan nestled in her pocket, and the loaf of bread and package of salt rested rested between two cloths in the shopping basket she carried. A gift of salt and bread was the Serbian tradition for a first visit to a home. She kissed Teta Lily and Zoran. Stefan took the basket from Miriana, opened both doors, and they stepped onto the snowy porch. As they went through the gate in the yard where Mama and Tata were tending the animals, they waved. "I already greeted them on the way in," Stefan said, reassuring Miriana.

"*Srechan Bozhich*, Merry Christmas, Stefan" they called to him, and waved back.

It was a crisp, cold day, and hard snow crunched underfoot as they walked side by side, in silence at first. Miriana was the first to speak. She described her Christmas Eve concluding with only a brief mention of the dress. "And you?" she asked.

"It was okay, I guess. Mama got out the photograph album, as she does every Christmas Eve. She looks at the photos of my dad, and she cries. I always feel sad for her when that happens. I miss *having* a father, but I can't say I really miss *him*. I never knew him. I was just two when he died. But do you know what is scary in all this?" Stefan didn't wait for an answer. "I look exactly like him. Every time I look at a photo of him, it's like looking at myself in a mirror. The same eyes, the same hair, the same dimples. Even my size. My mother comes to my shoulder, and that's exactly where she comes to him in the pictures: to my dad's shoulder. I guess I'm a little leaner, but he's older in the photos."

"What was his first name? Was it also 'Stefan'?"

"Of course! 'Stefan Stefanovich,' Stefan, son of Stefan. That's me. Isn't that the Serbian tradition?"

"What did he do, Stefan?" It occurred to Miriana just then that in all the years she had known Stefan, she hadn't learned much about his father. This was the most he had ever told her.

"He was a locksmith," Stefan replied, "but he stayed home to run the farm. He really liked it. And I guess that's why Mama wants me to stay home and be a farmer—besides the fact that right now they need the help."

He looked at Miriana. "We had a fight about it again last night. Can you believe it? On Christmas Eve. She can't even let up for one night." He stopped talking abruptly.

"Stefan." She put her hand on his arm, and they stopped walking. He turned to look at her. "Maybe Teta Lily can help. She is so in favour of education. She was the only woman lawyer to graduate from her class, you know. Maybe she could talk to your mother."

"Maybe," he said, and sighed.

"You're not giving up, are you?"

Stefan bristled. "Of course not!" he almost shouted. Then, more softly, he continued, "It's just that Chika Rajkovich has already spoken to her, and she won't budge. I don't see how your aunt can help."

"Well," Miriana said, "anything is worth a try, isn't it?"

"I suppose," he agreed. "Listen, Miriana, don't say anything about it at dinner, please. Don't even let her know I've discussed it with you."

She nodded. Stefan removed her hand from his arm and cupped it in his own hand. His calloused hand was hard, strong and warm. Miriana felt a surge of ... of what, she wasn't sure. It was new. She looked ahead as they walked, once again in silence.

Stefan's mother was waiting for them at the door when they arrived.

She's a pretty woman, Miriana thought. *In fact, she must have been beautiful once.* Her complexion was smooth and pale, like Teta Lily's, but there were dark circles under her eyes. Her hair, dark blonde, almost brown, was thick and pulled back from her face. The severity of the style emphasized the lines forming around her eyes and mouth. She was about six centimetres taller than Miriana, stockier and heavier. Her grey eyes brimmed with tears.

"*Bozhe, bozhe,* oh god," she cried. "Oh, Stefan, you won't believe what happened. Soldiers came. They took our food, all of the Christmas dinner, almost everything. They had guns. I was so frightened."

"Who were they, Mama?" Stefan asked.

She shrugged. "They weren't wearing uniforms. I couldn't say. Partisans? Royalists? Who knows? Who cares? The food's gone."

Stefan put his arm around his mother, trying to comfort her.

He looks awkward like that, Miriana thought, and she shifted her gaze to the floor.

"Mama, we have a guest," Stefan reminded his mother. "Let's invite her in. There must be something left. How about a traditional Serbian welcome? Do you have any *slatko*?"

"Oh, yes. Excuse me, Miriana. Please, take off your coat," Mrs. Stefanovich said. As she kissed her cheeks, Miriana detected the sweet scent of lavender soap. "Stefan, give Miriana some slippers and take her to the sitting room. I'll join you in a minute."

Miriana took the basket from Stefan and handed her the loaf of bread wrapped in cloth and salt. Mrs. Stefanovich took the loaf and squeezed Miriana's arm.

Stefan's grandparents were sitting quietly, waiting for the young people to join them. Miriana knew them, although not well, especially old Deda, Stefan's grandfather, who was still spry enough to walk at the corso. She bent over Deda and Baba and kissed each of them on their cheeks. In a few minutes, Stefan's mother arrived carrying a tray with glasses of water, a pot of jam, and five spoons. Each of them took a spoon, scooped out a mass of sticky plum jam, and washed it down with a glass of water.

As soon as he could politely excuse them from the company of the adults, Stefan invited Miriana to his bedroom, just off the living room, leaving the door wide open. The room was neat, just as she expected it to be, and sparsely furnished. There was a bright red, woven kilim carpet on the floor, a sturdy wooden bed, and a mirror. On the dresser sat a photo of his parents. Miriana stared at it, shocked at the strong resemblance Stefan had just described to her. Beside the photo, Stefan's violin lay in an open case.

"Stefan, would you play the violin for me?" she asked.

He looked at her thoughtfully. "Not today," he said.

Miriana was disappointed, and it must have shown on her face.

"Look, why don't you come to Chika Rajkovich's next time I have a lesson? You can listen then. I just don't want to play right now. Please try to understand."

She didn't understand, but she nodded anyway. Sometimes she didn't understand Stefan's behaviour at all, but she always accepted it.

Maybe that's why we're so close, she thought.

"Miriana, I have a gift for you. That's why I invited you to my room. I wanted to do it in private. These are for you." Stefan held out his hand, and in it, he coddled a pair of hair combs made of gold and white enamel with a delicate swirl in the metallic part. The shiny surface glinted in the soft light coming through the window.

Miriana looked from the combs to him. He was watching her closely, and his eyes had an intense green hue.

"Stefan, wherever did you get them? They're incredibly beautiful!"

"From Chika Rajkovich. I worked for them. They belonged to his mother, and he has no wife, no daughter, no one to wear them. Now, put them in. Here, look. There's a mirror."

She took the combs from his hand. They were still warm from his grip. She stood in front of the mirror over the dresser and pushed the combs into her thick hair.

I feel and look much older than fifteen, she thought as she peered at her reflection, her cheeks echoing the red of her dress.

Stefan nodded. "Wow. I … I … I had no idea …" he stammered. Abruptly, he changed the subject.

"C'mon. Mama will have found a bit of food for us somewhere. Let's go drink a toast to the end of this damned war."

"Wait," Miriana said. She reached into the pocket of her skirt and pulled out the socks. They seemed so insignificant beside his gift, and she felt embarrassed that she had nothing better to give him, "It's not much, Stefan. Not anything like these combs. But they'll keep you warm. Happy Christmas."

"I'd rather have socks than hair combs any day." He grinned. "Thanks, Miriana. Happy Christmas," he replied, brushing his lips lightly over hers.

CHAPTER 8

Death Comes Close to Home

LIFE AFTER CHRISTMAS WAS ANTICLIMACTIC. THE DRUDGERY of work and the bitterness of a cold winter had set in. Miriana attended school every day but felt as if she was hanging on by a tenuous thread. There was talk of closing the school.

By the time she came home, her mother, father and aunt were tired. Sometimes they were red and raw from work in the outdoors. Even Teta Lily's hands were coarse and cracked. The mill was closed in the coldest part of the winter, when the ice was frozen over the river and there was no power to turn the mill wheel, but there was always work to do. Tata spent his winter days in his shop, inside the mill, working on metal parts.

In the evening, at the first signs of darkness, they put up blackout curtains to seal off any light in the house. Orders. The town was to be in total darkness so that aircraft could not be guided to their targets by the glow of light emanating from town houses.

At night, they shuffled about with uncertainty in the dim flicker of a candle. Miriana studied at the kitchen table in the dimness, and she was often the last one ready for bed. The adults, exhausted from the day's work that started before the first hint of dawn, were usually in bed as soon as Zoran was asleep. Her father, especially, looked grey, and there were dark circles under his eyes.

The last week of January, a storm descended on them, and Miriana lay curled in her blankets, listening and watching to the storm rage. The wind howled and whined as air rushed through cracks in the window. Wet snow clung to corner of windows and doors in curvaceous patterns. The air in the house was cool and damp. Tata coughed in short staccato bursts as he had seemed to do every night for the last few weeks.

Miriana shivered, and not just from the cold. She thought about the conversation she had overheard this afternoon when she and Zoran were returning from feeding the animals.

They can't do it, she thought. *Surely, they won't still insist I stay home and work. Oh, I hope Teta Lily can persuade them to let me keep going to school—if it stays open. If I quit school now, I'll never be able to go to university.*

Stefan was right. Thank goodness, she had her aunt on her side. She was sure that Teta Lily was the only reason her parents had not made her quit long before now.

WHAM! Something outside knocked and crashed. Miriana started. *WHAM!* There it was again. She heard her father grunt and mumble something to her mother.

"Tata, what is it?" she called out.

"Don't know exactly," he replied, poking his head around the blanket wall. "Sounds like a door loose, maybe. I'm going out to see." He let the blanket fall back into place.

Miriana followed his movements by his sounds as he pulled shut each door behind him. She heard Teta Lily up.

"No, don't need any help. Don't know what it is yet," she heard Tata say.

"Mama?" Miriana called.

"Yes?" Mama stepped into Miriana's part of the bedroom. She was completely dressed. "Go to sleep, Sertse. I'm going to make some tea for your father. You need your rest."

Her father no longer coughed in the bed beside her, and once the banging stopped, Miriana felt herself drift off into sleep. She slept fitfully, unconscious of the passing of time. She was vaguely aware of hearing her parents return to bed, but she had no idea when that was. The coughing started again.

When morning came, Miriana felt tired, but she dragged herself from the bed and stumbled through her morning routine of dressing, combing and folding. As her head cleared, she became more aware of the coughing again.

Tata! Is he still in bed? Couldn't be. He is always up before me, she thought. She peeked around the blankets and saw her father, still in bed.

As if he sensed her presence, Tata lifted his head. "*Bozhe,* what time is it?" As he leaned forward, a cough racked his body.

"It's seven-thirty," Miriana answered, when he finally stopped coughing.

"I have to get to wo—" He inhaled deeply and involuntarily as the coughing once again seized his body.

Mama came into the bedroom. "Nikola, get back into bed. You can't work with this cold. I'll bring you some camomile tea." She turned to Miriana. "Hurry, Miriana. You have to ask Shasula to come today on your way to school."

Miriana did not complain. She was happy to hear the word "school." Every day was a step towards university in the city: a step towards a different life away from the drudgery of the mill. She rushed. Mama had made her a new dress for school so that the red one could be saved for special occasions. The new one, a coarse, blue wool shift, was rough and scratched her skin wherever it touched. Miriana hated the cloth, but at least it was loose and didn't hug her growing body as the old brown one had. And it was warm. She made some passes at her bushy hair with the brush, but she didn't check it in the mirror.

It will only blow in the wind anyway, she thought.

She was in the kitchen for breakfast in record time. Mama was already there, moving in her pattern that Miriana decided must be the closest thing to perpetual motion.

"What happened last night, Mama?" she asked and stuffed a slice of bread into her mouth.

"The wind ripped the door of the animal shelter off its hinges. It hadn't been closed properly. The door was hanging by only one metal strip and was banging in the wind. Your tata had to fix it before all the animals froze or wandered off."

"How long was he up?" Miriana washed down her crust of bread with a gulp of tea.

"Oh, I guess about three-quarters of an hour. He did a rough job. It needs to be fixed proper," her mother answered. "Are you ready to go already, Miriana? Shouldn't you have something more to eat?"

"No, Mama, I'm full. But yes, I'm ready to go. Where's Teta Lily?"

"Out in the yard with Zoran. Morning chores. Here, Sertsa, take your lunch, and don't forget to stop at Shasula's." She kissed Miriana's cheeks. Even her lips were rough, Miriana noticed.

Tata was in bed for the next four days. Sometimes he was feverish and sometimes chilled. He still coughed, and he had trouble breathing. He no longer protested at having to stay in bed, and he accepted meekly the tea and soup that Miriana, her aunt, or her mother took to him. Shasula came every day to help with Zoran and the household chores.

The weather was warming, and it looked as if spring would finally arrive. The ice on the stream was breaking up and the sounds of gurgling, gushing water greeted Miriana when she returned from school.

Soon the mill will be running again, she thought.

As she opened the door, she heard voices in the kitchen. She recognized her aunt and her mother. The third voice was a man's.

Thank goodness, it's not Atsa Teshki, she thought. *But who, then?*

A gust of wind slammed the door shut behind her, alerting the adults to her arrival. A man was sitting at the table sipping a cup of tea. Slender, with dark hair thinning at the flat spot on his head that identified him as Slavic, he looked to be in his forties. His brow furrowed over his elongated metal-framed spectacles, and his mouth was drawn back in a concise, controlled smile. The whiteness of his skin told Miriana he wasn't a labourer. She had a feeling of warmth and comfort that emanated from the man.

Teta Lily broke the silence that had fallen on the room. "Miriana, do you know Dr. Tedosevic?"

The doctor! Of course. She remembered him from church. And sometimes she would see him in town. But she had never been a patient, nor could she remember Mama or Tata ever visiting him either. So what was he doing here?

"Tata?" she blurted, "how is he?"

Mama was already bustling about the kitchen making more tea. The kettle shrieked on the stove, and the cups, the best ones, tinkled as her mother set them on their saucers. Mama stopped only to exchange glances with the doctor and Teta Lily.

"Tell her what you just told us," Teta Lily said to Dr. Tedosevic.

Dr. Tedosevic sat slumped in his chair and motioned to Miriana to sit down. She sat quietly, straining to hear, to understand. Mama splashed tea into her cup.

The doctor removed his glasses, rubbed his weary eyes with his thumb and first finger, and heaved a heavy sigh. He turned to meet Miriana's eyes. "Your father has pneumonia. There is little I can do for him. He needs a sulfa drug, and there are no drugs to be had. We can only give him lots of fluids, make him cool when he is hot, and make him warm when he is cold. And hope." The doctor stopped, and his chin dropped to his chest.

"What about Belgrade?" Teta Lily asked. "If I went there on the train, could I get some sulfa drugs there?"

Miriana's mother snorted. "Lily, have you lost your mind? This baby is due any day. You couldn't possibly go to Belgrade in your condition." She turned to the doctor and took a deep breath. Her voice softened. "But, Doctor, *can* we get some medicine in Belgrade?"

Miriana stared at one and then another as they spoke. She struggled to assimilate what they were saying. Was her father going to die? She thought about Stefan. He had lived since he was a baby without a father. But that was different. Her father was strong and alive. He lifted heavy loads with seemingly little effort every day. When she was little, he used to pick her up, hold her upside down so that her hair swept the floor, and call her "rag mop."

"Dear ladies," the doctor answered, "we Serbians have no antibiotics anywhere. They are simply not available. If I knew of a source, I would tell you. You have to do what you can to relieve the symptoms, and if you are religious, pray."

There was silence, and Miriana could hear the laboured breathing of her father in the next room.

"Wait a minute, Doctor," Teta Lily blurted, "you said the Serbians don't have any sulfa drugs. Do you mean that somebody else does?"

Dr. Tedosevic rose from the table. "I don't know. It's possible the Germans might have some for their officers. On the other hand, they might simply send sick men home to Germany. I can assure you, if they do have drugs, they won't be giving them to us. Please. I'll call back tomorrow to see how Nikola is doing. Mrs. Markovich, may I please have my coat?" Mama retrieved his coat from the hook.

Teta Lily stared pensively into space, chewing on her fist.

Miriana cleared the table like an automaton, her mind on her father and the conversation.

That night, she lay in her bed listening with concern to the coughing and the breathing of her father. She tossed and turned, unable to shake the gravity of the doctor's prognosis. By morning, she had made a decision: she was needed at home. School would just have to wait. She announced her decision after breakfast. Mama accepted the idea and seemed almost relieved, but Teta Lily was distraught.

"Sertse," she implored, "think of what you are doing. I know how important an education is to you."

"It's just for a while, Teta Lily," Miriana responded, "I can catch up later. And I can ask Stefan to bring me work to do at home in the evenings." She rubbed a dirty pot she had been cleaning with renewed determination. She hoped she could hold her resolve.

Teta Lily sighed. Miriana scrubbed harder. She felt as if she had betrayed her aunt.

The doctor came, as promised, just before dinner. Mama went into the bedroom with him while Teta Lily and Miriana waited in the kitchen with Zoran. Nobody spoke. Even Zoran sat wordlessly, twisting a length of yarn around a colourful piece of cloth he used to tease the cats.

When Dr. Tedosevic emerged from the bedroom, Teta Lily and Miriana stood up hopefully, but he just shook his head. "He's just the same, and I can do nothing more. Put some hot steaming water in his room when he seems to have trouble catching his breath."

The doctor bundled himself in his heavy winter clothing. Mama handed him a bag of flour that he accepted and tucked under his arm. "Is it enough?" she asked.

"It's more than enough, Mrs. Markovich. I wish I could be more helpful," he said, laying a hand on her shoulder.

He pulled open the door; a tall, red-cheeked young man stood with his arm raised, ready to knock, blocking his exit. With some embarrassment, Stefan lowered his arm and stepped aside so that the doctor could pass. Miriana bounded to the door, took Stefan's hand, and pulled him in before he could change his mind. He followed the departing figure with his eyes for just an instant before turning to Miriana.

"That was the doctor," Stefan said, almost matter-of-factly. But it was really a question.

"Stefan, come and sit down. You look frozen," Teta Lily said. "Can you stay for supper? It's almost ready."

"Oh, no, thank you, Mrs. Lowenthal. My mother has dinner waiting for me, and then I have to practise, do chores, and do homework. I just came by because Miriana was not at school today." He stopped, but Miriana knew by the way his eyebrows curved high on his forehead that there were questions to be answered.

"Tata's still ill. The doctor says he has pneumonia," Miriana told him.

Stefan's brows dropped as she talked. Miriana watched as the high, sleek lines became knitted at the centre and bristled at the outer ends.

What's he thinking, she wondered. *Is he thinking of his own father?* She felt her chest tighten as if someone had put a tight band around it. She had a glimpse of what Stefan's loss might be like. Her own father lay close to death, and she was powerless to help.

"Is there anything I can do?" Stefan offered.

"Yes, could you please bring homework from school for me? Take notes of what has to be done, and drop it off here every night after class?" Miriana asked.

"You mean, you're not coming back?" Stefan's voice rose in a crescendo of disbelief.

"I don't know. Yes, well, maybe. Someday, when Tata gets better."

Miriana watched Stefan's eyes grow dark. There was a storm brewing in him, and she knew he disapproved. There were now two against her decision. It had been hard enough without more pressure.

"Your stable door needs mending," he mumbled. "I noticed it hanging crookedly when I arrive. I'll be along tomorrow to fix it."

"Oh Stefan, you don't have time to do that," Teta Lily protested. "You have your studies, your violin, and chores of your own."

"That's all right Mrs. Lowenthal. I can manage. Besides, if I don't do it, who will do it for you?" Stefan retorted.

"He's right, Teta Lily," Miriana defended Stefan.

Teta Lily sighed. "It's just that I want you young people to have opportunities in life. Maybe I'm trying to shield you too much from this damn war. Okay, Stefan. That's very generous of you. And you're right. The door needs mending, and we can't do it. Thank you. Are you sure you can't stay for supper?"

"Yes, I'm sure, and no, I can't, but thanks. I have to go now. I'll see you tomorrow." Stefan held Miriana's eyes with his for an instant, flicked a glance at Teta Lily, reddened, and slipped out the door.

"Such a sensitive, kind guy," Teta Lily commented. "So shy."

"My best friend," Miriana murmured, wondering, since that little kiss at Christmas, if maybe there was more.

Two days passed, and her father continued to weaken. Mama spent most of her time caring for him. Miriana divided her time between helping in the house, caring for Zoran, and looking after the livestock. Stefan came by, not only the next day but every day. He helped with chores that were too strenuous for the women. He brought schoolwork home for Miriana, but she was generally too tired in the evening to do it.

The doctor also stopped by to check on Miriana's father, but he always left the same despair. Teta Lily questioned the doctor at length about drugs. He would answer politely but shake his head and shrug his shoulders.

Ten days after the evening when Tata fell ill, Miriana heard the familiar growl of a German truck as it pulled into the yard.

Oh god, she thought, *what next? Poor Teta Lily is tired from working all day. She doesn't need this.*

Miriana looked over at her aunt; she was stooped over measuring flour into a sack, but she must have heard the truck too. Teta Lily stood up slowly, and when she finally reached her full height, she placed her hands on her back for support, scrunching up her face as she waited for the soreness in her body to go away and the soldier to approach. Her face and hands were coated with white flour, and there were patches of dirt on her dress where she had been kneeling. A white scarf wrapped around her head barely contained and controlled her thick brown hair that had worked itself loose from hours of work. Strands of dark hair coated in the white flour made her look as if she were starting to turn grey.

Miriana recognized the soldier and reddened at the thought of seeing him. It was Hans, and he was alone. Even though she didn't understand everything that was said between Teta Lily and Hans, she guessed that it was for the same thing and waited patiently for her aunt to explain.

"I'll have to go, Miriana," she said. "It's the usual translation. Can you please give Zoran dinner and put him to bed if I'm not back on time?"

"Of course. Are you going to change first, Teta Lily?"

Her aunt laughed. "Is it that bad? I'll just wash my face and hands first. Miriana, this could be a blessing in disguise," Teta Lily said mysteriously. She kissed Miriana's forehead and waddled to the pump to wash up.

Miriana turned back to her work, eager to avoid looking at Hans. The memory of his last visit burned in her mind. She could smell the same metallic cologne and wasn't sure whether it was real or imagined. The tension of Josif in the cellar and Zoran's insistence on opening that door had made her tremble.

Why doesn't he leave? she thought. *I can't look at him.* She busied herself with tying the bag, and she was grateful for the strands of hair that became loose and hung protectively over her burning cheeks.

"Hello, Miriana," he said, in heavily accented Serbian. "You ... you ... you are pretty."

Surprised, and in spite of herself, Miriana looked up. Hans's gaze was fixed on her, but she couldn't read anything in his expression. His eyes were intensely blue in this light, but he was neither smiling nor frowning. Suddenly, he turned on his heel and left Miriana gawking at his broad, straight back.

She knotted the last sack furiously and went inside to help her mother start dinner.

Darn, him, she thought. She kept thinking of Hans, and she felt puzzled and angry. What made her feel so agitated?

By the time Miriana got Zoran ready for bed and helped her mother wash up, it was nearly dark. They left some soup simmering on the stove for Teta Lily, and the aroma of potatoes and onions permeated the room. As they put up the blackout curtains, Miriana worried about Teta Lily. She was really late. What would happen if the curfew came into effect before her aunt got home?

They lit the candles in the kitchen, and Miriana looked at the schoolwork that was piling up. It made her feel guilty. Maybe tonight she would have enough energy to do some. She was tired and wanted to fall asleep, but she was determined to stay awake until Teta Lily returned. She worked in fits and starts, losing her concentration and then regaining it, nibbling away at the work like a person full of food might tackle a second meal. Finally, as the sky became grey before black, she heard the roar of an engine. It must be Teta Lily. Carefully, she lifted the curtain over the window to peer outside. It was.

Thank god, Miriana thought.

Teta Lily opened the door, stepped in, and meticulously closed the door behind her and locked it.

"I got it!" she blurted. "I got it!"

"What? What did you get, Lily?" Mama dried her hands on her apron and put her arm around her sister. The look on her face showed her confusion.

Teta Lily fumbled with her coat, hat and gloves. She tossed them on a chair and riffled the voluminous pocket of her smock. Her face was tense and pale, her lips drawn back in a terse smile. Her hands fluttered nervously, and after a few seconds, she produced a brown glass bottle filled with liquid.

"It's sulfa," she whispered, "for Nikola."

"Oh my god, Lily! How did you … where did you …? Oh Lily! This is the gift of life! But …" Miriana's mother stammered.

"Militsa, Miriana," Teta Lily said looking from one to the other, "you must never tell anyone about this. I got it from the German medic centre, but I won't tell you more than that. Swear you won't tell anyone."

"I promise. But, oh Lily, how can we ever thank you?" Mama cried. Tears trickled the length of her nose.

Miriana hugged her aunt. "You are a miracle worker. What would we ever do without you?"

"What would I ever do without you?" Teta Lily answered, and hugged her back. "Now, I have directions. Let's start Nikola on this right away," she said, releasing Miriana and rushing to the drawer for a spoon.

Miriana took a deep breath and blew it out slowly. She felt her shoulders start to relax.

Tata, you have to get better, she thought. *You just have to.*

CHAPTER 9

Hope
February 1943

W ITH HER FATHER RECOVERING FROM HIS PNEUMONIA
and working for short periods, life was restoring to
normal—at least, to the new normal for Miriana. Mama worked in
the mill with Tata, and Teta Lily, whose baby was already overdue,
looked after the household chores. Miriana returned to school. Teta
Lily insisted on it, and Stefan was pleased that Miriana was back. No
one was happier about that than Miriana. Catching up was work, real
work, after the long time away.

The day started off as any other day, and it would have been a good
day if it hadn't been for Olga.

It shouldn't be "Pandora's box"; it should be "Olga's box," Miriana
thought as she trudged along beside Stefan. *If someone at that school is
going to cause trouble, it's always Olga Bogdanovich.* Aloud, she said to
Stefan, "Why did she ask me all those questions?"

"Oh, don't listen to her, Miriana. You know she is jealous of you because you do well at school and she doesn't. She just wants to hurt you," Stefan replied.

"Why did she have to pick on my father? Tata works so hard. And he's a good man. If someone can't afford to pay, he always does the work for free. He took in my aunt and that young—" She was thinking of Josif but realized she shouldn't say that. "He never asks for anything for himself."

"What exactly did she say about your father?" he asked.

"She kept asking me questions about why my father wasn't a soldier. She wanted to know why he wasn't fighting in the war. 'Only men who are too old, too sick, or cowards stay home when there is a war,' she said." Miriana paused. "Stefan, I never thought about it before. I don't know why my father is home instead of fighting. I do know he's not any of those things Olga insinuated. What do you think?"

"I told you. Don't listen to her—or anybody else. I can't wait until this damn war is over. Did you see those little guys playing in the yard today? They were playing war, shooting one another and blowing up one another. One of them even said, 'I just blew off your arm and half your face.' And look at the Damjanovich brothers. They went off at seventeen and eighteen, and now they are both dead. It's gruesome, Miriana. They're romanticizing man's animal nature. Don't let Olga bother you. Ignore her and everyone else."

"I guess you're right, Stefan. Still, it bothers me to know that she thinks that way and that she is cruel enough to say it," Miriana replied.

They were already at the gate to Miriana's yard. There was a bicycle leaning against the fence.

"You have company," Stefan commented. He spotted Zoran playing in the yard near his Uncle Nikola and waved to him.

"I don't recognize the bike. I don't know who it could be, but I guess I'll soon find out. I'll tell you tomorrow. Bye, Stefan," she said with a half smile, and she climbed the steps to the house.

Even though Stefan had told her to ignore Olga's remarks, she couldn't get them out of her head, and she certainly couldn't tell her parents.

No one was in the kitchen. The house seemed quiet.

Where are Mama and Teta Lily, she thought. Then she heard voices in the bedroom. "Mama?" she called. "Mama, are you there?" She knocked softly on the bedroom door.

Her mother opened it, and Miriana could see Teta Lily on the bed, a sheet drawn over her. She was breathing heavily, her brow drawn into a tight frown, her eyes focused on something at the end of the bed.

Miriana didn't recognize the heavy-set, robust-looking woman who was bending over her aunt. She had a ruddy complexion, and her face was so smooth and scrubbed that her skin glistened. It was her hands that attracted Miriana. They were clean, long for the size of the rest of her, and strong.

"The baby's coming," Mama whispered. "The midwife is here. Why don't you go out in the yard and play with Zoran? He's with your father. I'll call you when the baby's born."

Miriana nodded, and her mother closed the door.

The baby! She felt strangely excited. She hadn't thought much about the arrival of this new little baby since the first days, when she was sure it was going to be terrible to have two young children in the house. She had already forgotten about ugly Olga and went to find Zoran.

They fed the animals and played with the cats, everything they loved to do, but Miriana found herself glancing impatiently at the door to the house.

Zoran tugged at her skirts eagerly. "C'mon, Yanna, I wanna see kitties."

She allowed herself to be dragged into the shed where one of the cats had just given birth to a litter of kittens. She looked at the helpless heap of moving fur; she was going to pick up one when she heard her mother call. She bounded to her feet, grabbed Zoran by the hand, and scooted out of the barn with Zoran flying behind her.

Mama stood grinning on the porch. "It's a girl," she said. "Zoran, you have a little sister."

"I wanna see baby!" Zoran shrieked. "Can I play with her?"

"You go wash up at the pump, and you can come in and see her," Mama promised. "Zoran, you are a big brother. How would you like to go tell your uncle Nikola that you have a little sister? He doesn't know yet."

"Okay," he yelled, and tore away from Miriana's grip.

"Techa Nik'la! Techa Nik'la!" he yelled, running across the yard.

Miriana watched her father pick up Zoran in his muscular arms and carry him to the pump where she waited. She pumped vigorously, splashing water on her face and hands. She helped Zoran wash and then tiptoed into the house. Zoran tore in ahead of her in a burst of chatter, his hard shoes knocking on the wooden floor.

The door to the bedroom was open. Teta Lily reclined against two pillows, smiling. Zoran ran to her and threw his arms around her. "Where baby, Mama? Did it come out of your tummy?"

Before Teta Lily could answer, the baby howled. The sound came from the kitchen, not the bedroom. Miriana turned her head. There, on the table, was a small red-faced baby with fine blonde hair. The baby hollered and kicked as the midwife worked hastily, washing her and wrapping her in a cloth nightie.

"Oh, look at her. She's so tiny!" Miriana remarked, in a stage whisper. She was struck by the diminutive detail of every human feature.

Teta Lily called the midwife. "Please bring the baby in here for the children to see."

The infant looked fragile against the massive frame of the midwife. Tenderly, the woman lowered her arms, and Miriana peered at the small, blonde head and pink, wrinkled face, all she could see of the swaddled baby.

"Do you want to hold her?" Teta Lily asked Miriana.

Miriana nodded and took the baby nervously into her arms. How light, warm and delicate she felt! She leaned her cheek against the infant's, feeling the softest skin she had ever touched and smelling a fresh, sweet perfume that she could only describe as "baby." Miriana cuddled and rocked her until Zoran grabbed at the baby.

"Me! Me wanna hold baby!" he yelled. The midwife held his arms so that he could not tear at the baby's clothing.

"Zoran, I need you to hug *me*," his mother said. "You will have a turn to hold the baby in a minute."

The baby stirred in Miriana's arms. She made mewing noises and turned her head towards Miriana. Her lips puckered, and she sucked on Miriana's dress.

"What's she doing?" Miriana gasped.

"I would say that's a hungry baby," her mother replied, laughing. "She wants to nurse."

"Oh," was all Miriana could manage to reply. She wasn't quite sure what to do now. The midwife made the decision for her by taking the baby from her and depositing her in Teta Lily's arms.

"What's her name?" Miriana asked, still staring at the little face.

"Nada. Do you like it? It means hope," her aunt answered.

"Oh, yes, I do."

Nada. Yes, that's a good name, Miriana thought. *Hope.*

CHAPTER 10

Under Attack
May 1943

MIRIANA BENT OVER THE SLOP PAIL. IT DIDN'T SMELL TOO bad on a cool May morning, not like it did in the summer heat. In the hot months, kitchen garbage sometimes reeked by the next morning.

"Come on, Zoran," Miriana said. "Time to take breakfast to Pasha and Ali Beg. Just because you have a full tummy doesn't mean everyone else should starve. Get your sweater on, and let's go."

She helped Zoran pull on his heavy sweater and fasten the buttons. He didn't need any encouragement to go into the yard. Miriana slipped on her own sweater without bothering to do it up.

They took the pail between them, Miriana pretending that Zoran was carrying the pail and she was only helping him. The pail was heavy, even when it was empty. Zoran huffed and grunted with the effort. His face took on a serious expression. He clenched his teeth, puffed his ruddy cheeks, and lowered his brow with the strain. His little body bowed over to the side, and he walked as if one leg were shorter than the other. Miriana smiled at his determination.

"Who will we feed first?" she asked.

Zoran was quiet for a moment while he thought. "Uhhh ... Pasha," he replied.

They thudded the pail down the wooden steps and lifted it for the last little trek to the dumping ground. "*Hunh*," Zoran grunted as he released it on a bare spot beside the pen. Already the two pigs knew that the food was coming, and they were running with a waddle to the fence. Their wrinkled, pink snouts dripped with mucus, and they pointed them in the direction of the food. At the fence, they stopped, snorting and screeching.

"Morning, piggy," Zoran said to each of them. He grabbed the rails of the pen with his hands and went down on his knee so that he could reach between the posts to stroke them. The pigs grunted impatiently while he caressed their fat, round, pink bodies studded with prickly bristles of hair. Their mouths never seemed to stop. Miriana took the pail by herself and poured the contents into the empty wooden trough. A slimy mixture of eggshells, potato and carrot peelings, pepper seeds, apple cores and turnip pieces slithered out of the pail and plopped into the pigs' bowl. The pigs shoved their noses into the slop and chomped at food before Miriana had finished pouring. The last few pieces landed on their heads and slid between their ears and down their snouts.

"They hungry," Zoran shouted, standing up.

"Of course, lazy!" Miriana said with a laugh. "It's already late. You kept them waiting this morning."

They leaned against the fence, watching the pigs eat. The sound of the gristmill whirred steadily in the background, and the pigs grunted and snorted as they pushed the food around hungrily. The pungent odour of pigs was almost overpowering, even outside.

Miriana turned around to pick up the rest of the scraps. The large tom turkey had his head buried in the scraps and was pecking away.

"Hey!" Miriana shouted, "you have to share that!" She shooed him away from the bucket with her hand. The old tom strutted away regally, holding his head high and looking down his beak imperiously, his comb swaying and his feathers puffing.

"We feed others," Zoran said. He grabbed the handle and dragged the pail across the yard to the poultry shed. His cheeks were becoming ruddy with the cold, and his knees below his short grey woollen trousers were two red knobs.

The fowl ran around freely in the yard. Most of them were timid, nervous creatures that would scurry away with a jerk and a squawk. Only the tom turkey was bold enough to approach them. Miriana had named him *Kralj* because he acted like his name: King.

She helped Zoran dump the rest of the scraps around the coop. "I'm going for the grain now," she said to Zoran. He was already bent over, hugging his knees and talking to the glassy-eyed birds as they fought and pecked one another for the food. "Do you want to come?" Zoran slipped his hand into hers and broke into a clumsy skip.

Miriana's father kept a scoop hanging on a nail on the wall at the side of the mill. Miriana used it to scoop up some of the grain lying on the wooden floor of the mill into the bucket. Dust rose in the air, making Zoran sneeze. Grain crunched under their hard-soled shoes.

Miriana's parents were hard at work. Tata was pouring grain into a chute above the millstones and collecting flour in large bags at the base of another chute. Even though it was a cool day, sweat streaked down his face. Mama weighed the flour and divided it into two bags. Ten percent of the flour was theirs to keep in return for grinding the flour, and the remainder was returned to the farmer.

"Tata, we came for grain for the birds," Miriana said, pointing to the bucket. Her father leaned on his shovel with one hand and swiped at the dribbling sweat with the other.

"Miriana, please, go to the pump and bring me some water."

"Only after I finish with the chickens," she said, with a toss of her hair. She looked at him seriously for a second, and then she could hold it back no longer: she burst into laughter and ran off with the pail before her father could cuff her affectionately.

Zoran bolted after her. He took handfuls of grain and scattered it over the hard-packed dirt of the yard. The chickens were anxious to start pecking, and they strutted about nervously behind them. Whenever Zoran and Miriana changed direction suddenly, the birds turned to flee with a cluck leaving delicate, downy white feathers flying in their wake.

"Zoran, I'm going to the house to get a cup for Uncle Nikola. You stay here and finish spreading the grain."

Zoran hardly seemed to notice as he flung grain awkwardly with his soft, round hands. Miriana left him with the bucket while she went into the house. The aroma of baking came from the kitchen.

"*Ummm.* Smells delicious, Teta Lily. What is it?" Miriana asked as she sucked in the sweetish smells and the warmth of the kitchen.

"Nut cake," her aunt replied, kneading dough. "Have you ever had it before?"

"No, I don't think so. How is it made?"

"Sugar, eggs, ground nuts, raisins, vanilla, lemon, semolina. Would you like to learn how to make it?"

"Yes, please. I would love to bake, but Mama is so busy helping Tata at the mill that she seldom has time to bake and even less time to teach me anything."

"Well, we're out of sugar now and I doubt there will be any more for quite some time. Miriana, where is Zoran?" Teta Lily asked, stopping her kneading.

"He's still out with the chickens. Sometimes I think he likes the animals more than he likes anyone else here!"

Teta Lily laughed. "That's just because he didn't have them in the city. It's still a special treat for him."

"I'll finish in the yard and then—"

"Oh my god. *Bozhe, bozhe.* Airplanes!" Teta Lily bolted for the door. She wrenched it open with her sticky, floured hands.

Miriana could hear the roar of the engines. They were coming closer and fast. It sounded as if they were almost overhead. She rushed to the door behind Teta Lily. She could see one plane flying low over an adjacent lot. The next one behind was on its way over their yard. It barely cleared the rooftops and trees, its grey-green body attacking angrily through the air like a shark in for the kill.

"Zoran!" Teta Lily called as loudly as she could without screaming. "Zoran, lie down." She crouched in the doorway of the house. "Zoran!" she called again.

Miriana could see Zoran in the yard by the water pump. He stared at the aircraft, watching their bullets pelt the dirt with a *puft-puft-puft* sound. The sandy soil shot up like miniature geysers. Zoran's eyes were round and wide. He stood with his chin turned to the sky, his arms dangling at his sides.

Oh my god, Miriana thought.

"ZORAN!" Teta Lily screamed this time.

Zoran turned and looked at her.

"Zoran, lie down. On your tummy. Behind the rain barrel."

He just looked at her. She tried again.

"Zoran, lie down. On your tummy.

Zoran dropped to his hands and knees and flattened himself against the ground.

"Good boy; stay there. Don't move until Mama tells you," she shouted.

Miriana watched wordlessly as Teta Lily directed Zoran from the stoop of the house. She wondered how much Zoran heard over the noise of the aircraft. The planes kept coming, and the lines of bullets came with them, leaving pockmarks in the soil.

Zoran was obedient. He stayed down as Teta Lily, bent over in a crouch against the house, and Miriana, squatting in the doorway behind her, watched him nervously.

The din was so loud that the sound of the mill was completely drowned out. Miriana felt choked, her stomach knotted. She gripped her hands tightly in her lap until the roar of the planes became so unbearable she clapped her sweaty palms over her ears.

It seemed endless, lines of planes roaring overhead, their bullets strafing the earth, chickens scurrying about the yard with no direction.

Finally, the dust geysers stopped, and the roar of motors faded. It could only have lasted a few minutes, but it seemed interminable. Miriana's hands were shaking, and she could barely stand up. Teta Lily ran across the yard and scooped Zoran into her arms. He was dusty and dirty, but he was alive. She held him tightly against her chest, tears running down her cheeks.

One of the pigs had been hit. Miriana saw a rush of blood where the flesh was ripped apart. It was Pasha. He screamed shrilly. His legs collapsed beneath him, and he crashed to the ground. He lay there, his chest heaving, blood oozing from the red blotch on his side.

From the porch, Miriana saw her father and mother running from the mill.

Her father shouted to her, "Miriana, are you all right?"

All she could do was nod.

Teta Lily carried Zoran to the veranda and sat rocking him in her arms, her face pale. Zoran sat passively for a minute, his eyes darting around the yard. Suddenly he wrenched himself from his mother's arms and ran across the yard to where two chickens lay bleeding on the ground.

"Yanna, c'mere. Look at Pile, the chickie," he called to Miriana. He stroked their feathers carefully, crooning. "Pile, Pile, what matter? Why you lying down? You hurt?"

"Militsa!" Miriana's father grunted, "Come help me with this pig. He's been hit bad." They lifted the pig from the pen and carried it between them to the shed.

"Where you going? What wrong with Pasha?" Zoran ran to the pen. "Why you carry him like that? You hurt him," Zoran yelled. His brow furrowed.

"He's in pain, Zoran," Teta Lily said. "He's hurt. A bullet hit him. Just like the chickens. Uncle Nikola will take away his pain. And we still have Ali Beg, the other pig. He will be here for you to feed tomorrow. C'mon, let's go see how Miriana and Nada are doing. Do you know what? I was just going to teach Miriana how to make nut cake. Do you—"

"Hey, Nada crying!" Zoran blurted. He raced to the door rushing past Miriana to the cradle. "Da-dum, da-dum," he rocked the cradle on its uneven runners the way his mama had shown him to do to settle Nada when she cried. "Sh, Nada, sh. Mama coming."

Miriana stood between the two scenes, not knowing where to turn until she felt an arm around her shoulders.

"Come on, Sertse, let's go in," Teta Lily said. "Your parents will look after the disaster out here, and you and I need to keep some sense of normalcy for Zoran. Can you please take the baby while I finish this mess?" she asked.

Miriana nodded. She picked up Nada and held her to her chest. The baby's head bobbed against her neck a few times, and she began sucking furiously at whatever her lips touched.

"I think she's hungry, Teta Lily," Miriana said.

"Bounce her a bit. I'll just wash up," her aunt replied.

"I hold her, I hold her, can I?" Zoran queried, jumping up and down.

"Not now, Zoran. Wait until she's been fed and changed. Here, you take some of that dough and roll it out flat." His mother gave him a lump of the sticky dough, finished wiping her hands on the towel, and took the baby from Miriana. She didn't coo and cluck today as she usually did when she was about to put the baby to her breast, Miriana noticed. She watched her aunt plop onto the sofa in the small sitting room and prop up her feet.

She looks tired, Miriana thought as her aunt settled the baby against her bosom.

There was only a minute of quiet. Miriana heard boots thud on the stoop. The door crashed open, and Stefan, panting and perspiring, burst into the kitchen. His black curls drooped against his glossy forehead that dripped with sweat. His chest heaved with heavy breathing.

Miriana's heart skipped a beat. "Stefan, are you all right? Your mother? Your grandparents?" She stared at his face, looking for answers.

Stefan nodded, still trying to catch his breath.

"I came … as fast … as … I could. Your parents?" He panted between words. Stefan looked down at Zoran rolling dough on the flour-dusted board and back to Miriana.

"Yes, we're fine," she replied. "Just a couple of chickens. And Pasha got hit. Tata and Mama are out cleaning up. What about the neighbours?"

"I don't know yet. I can't stay. I wish I could help, but we lost a sheep, and I have to go help my mother. I just came by to see how you are. There were no sirens this time, no warning. They caught us by surprise. Luckily, we were in the shed."

"Zoran was outside. In the yard," Miriana whispered. "Teta Lily had to guide him from the house to get him to lie down."

"Oh god!" Stefan gasped. He looked again at little Zoran who was perforating the slab of dough with his finger and roaring like an aircraft.

"*Puft, puft, puft*," Zoran exclaimed, with each little jab of his finger.

"God damn war," Stefan said, spinning on his heel and heading towards the door.

He almost bumped into Atsa Teshki who was on his way in. Miriana's face fell.

CHAPTER 11

Dragan

Another Serbian soldier came to hide in the cellar of the Markovich home. It had been stressful having Josif there, but he had been co-operative, and Atsa Teshki made a strong case for taking in another. They would be saving his life after all. Atsa promised it would just be a few days. No more than a week, he assured them.

Like Josif, the second soldier arrived in the dark of night. Miriana knew little about the man, just that his name was Dragan. She didn't meet him until the next day at suppertime when she had to take his tray downstairs, as she had done for Josif.

Dragan was a middle-aged man; Miriana didn't feel the same shock when she first saw him as she had with Josif. She had difficulty deciding how much over forty he was. Dragan was a swarthy man with a mat of black hair and a heavy, dark stubble of whiskers on a deeply lined face. The skin around his eyes was puffy, and small growths that looked like warts to Miriana dotted his face. His eyes, what she could see of them, were deep brown. She couldn't tell how tall he was because he was sitting, but he was a heavyset man, broad in the chest and rotund in the belly. White spittle formed at the corners of his lips, drawn tight while he sucked on the stub of a cigarette he held between yellow fingertips. The air reeked with the stench of cigarette smoke and his pungent body odour.

Miriana put the tray on the makeshift table.

"Thanks," he said. "What's your name?" he asked as Miriana started up the stairs.

She glanced at him. "Miriana," she replied simply. She didn't want to start a conversation with this man. He made her feel uncomfortable.

Please don't let him ask any more questions, she pleaded silently.

"Yeah," he said, and Miriana darted up the stairs.

Miriana took Dragan his meals whenever her mother asked her to do it, but she never stayed and talked with this man. He didn't seem to notice her, and he never said anything except to thank her. The tension of having a soldier hide in the cellar returned, and Miriana dreaded the thought of German soldiers coming for Teta Lily to translate, or of Zoran finding out about Dragan. With the good weather, Zoran played outdoors more, and it was easier to distract him.

Thank goodness, Miriana thought.

After six days, Dragan was still in the cellar, and there was no news from Atsa Teshki as to when Dragan would be leaving. There wasn't much the family could do. Once they accepted to hide the soldier, they became guilty too. Miriana tried not to think about it.

On Saturday, Miriana's parents went to work in the mill as usual. Teta Lily took Zoran to do the marketing, and Miriana volunteered to stay with Nada. She wanted to do some homework, and she knew that she could work at it while Nada slept. She had only one concern: what would she do if the German soldiers came looking for Teta Lily?

"You could give him a cold drink and ask him to wait outside,"

Teta Lily answered. "He can sit on the stoop. The weather is warm and sunny. He'll be comfortable."

Miriana nodded her consent nervously. It seemed like a plan that would work.

The house was quiet, and Miriana finished most of her work before Nada woke up. At noon, she put the baby on a blanket on the floor so that Nada could watch her prepare lunch.

"You like being able to see what's going on, don't you, Nada?"

Nada gurgled and shook her fists. Miriana loved to watch her.

"Time to take lunch to Dragan, Nada. I hope you don't have to do this when you are my age. I hope there is no war when you are sixteen." Nada cooed, and Miriana laughed.

"Just wait, Nada. I'll take this tray downstairs, and I'll be right back. You wait for me here. Oh, and Nada, don't tell anyone about Dragan, okay? Can you believe his name means 'dear'? I can't imagine him as a cute little baby, like you, but I guess his mother must have thought so when she named him." Miriana picked up the tray.

Halfway down the stairs, a new smell assailed Miriana. It was familiar, but she couldn't identify it for a moment.

What is it? she wondered.

Dragan was sitting in his usual spot, but instead of holding a cigarette, he held a bottle by the neck. Miriana recognized the bottle, and, at the same time, she identified the funky odour. Plum brandy. Dragan had found Tata's plum brandy, and he had been drinking it.

Hurriedly, she put the tray down, but before she could turn away, Dragan grabbed her wrist.

"It's some quiet up there," he said, his words slurring together. "Where's your father and mother?"

"They're at the mill. Working," Miriana replied. She was trembling.

"And auntie? Where's she?"

"You're drunk," said Miriana. "Let go of my wrist. You're hurting me."

"I just had a little drink," he said. "C'mere. Sit here on my lap, and spend a few minutes with me. It gets awful lonely down here sometimes." Dragan hiccoughed, and the overpowering odour of plum brandy took on a sour tinge.

"Dragan, please let me go. I left the baby alone upstairs."

"In a minute," he drawled. He put his arm around her waist and forced her to sit in his lap. Now she could smell nicotine too, and it made her queasy. He let go of her wrist, buried his nose in her hair and inhaled deeply. "You smell so sweet," he said.

Miriana was shaking. She tried to stand up, but he was strong and she felt his arm tighten around her middle. Slowly, one hand crept down her tummy and the other grabbed onto her breast.

"Let go! Let go," she screamed.

Dragan let go of her breast and clamped his hand instead over her mouth. Miriana began to panic. She kicked her feet and flailed her one free arm, but he just held on. Suddenly, with a quick jerk of the body, Dragan flipped her over onto her back. Miriana turned her head to the side so that she didn't have to look at his face or smell his foul breath. She could hear Nada wailing upstairs. Dragan had to reposition his hand covering her mouth, and when he let go, she screamed.

Will anybody hear me? she wondered. Dragan's mouth came down on hers, stifling her shrieks. The smell of him made her feel sick, and the weight of his body on hers left her fighting for breath.

She cried, tears running down her cheeks silently, her body shaking under his heft. She could feel the hardness in his trousers pushing against her.

There was a noise upstairs. Footsteps? Miriana tried to control her crying so that she could hear. Someone was up there. What can I do to alert whoever is there?

What if it's a German soldier? she thought. *That could be worse!* She sobbed. Dragan continued to paw her and kiss her. She couldn't move. A button popped off her dress where he forced his hand inside.

The door upstairs opened. "Miriana? Are you down there?" a voice called.

Stefan! Oh, thank god, it's him, Miriana thought.

"Miriana?" the voice called again.

Dragan must have heard the voice too. He let go of Miriana and rolled over, releasing her.

"Here, Stefan. Help me," she cried.

Stefan bounded down the stairs. "What's happening? The baby's shrieking upstairs—" The expression on his face changed when he saw her. "Miriana, are you okay?"

Miriana saw Stefan's eyes travel her body.

I must be a mess, she thought. His eyes stopped at the gape in the bodice of the dress. Miriana remembered that the button had come off, and she grabbed at the bodice of her dress self-consciously. Stefan helped her to her feet and embraced her. She shook in his arms and couldn't find the strength to answer.

"What were you trying to do?" Stefan shouted at Dragan. His face was scarlet.

"Oh, I was just tryin' to have a little kiss. Nothing important, see," Dragan leered. He put the bottle to his mouth and took a swig.

Stefan grabbed at the bottle, but Dragan was strong and he held on.

"No!" said Miriana. "Let him have it until he passes out. Please, Stefan, let's just get out of here."

Stefan put his arm around her waist and helped her up the stairs. She felt weak in the legs, and she was grateful for his help.

In the kitchen, Nada was crying so hard her face was purple. Miriana picked her up and held her against her shoulder, but Nada didn't stop crying. Miriana felt weak and like a baby herself. She wished someone would hug her and rock her. The tears continued to trickle.

"I'm going to get your father, Miriana. Is he at the mill?"

She nodded. Then, panicking at the thought of being left alone in the house, alone with that brute, she yelled and grabbed Stefan around the neck. "No! Don't leave me." Clutching Nada with one arm and Stefan with the other, she sobbed against his shoulder.

Stefan sighed and put his arm around her. "Miriana, I have to get someone. Who is that man? What's he doing here?"

The door opened, and Teta Lily stepped in. "Hello!" she called, in a questioning voice that trailed off when she looked up and saw the three of them standing in a huddle, two of them bawling.

Stefan reddened. He dropped his arms and shoved his hands in his pants pockets.

Teta Lily took Nada from Miriana. Her eyes fell to the gaping bodice on Miriana's dress. Miriana grabbed the two segments and pulled them together.

"What's going on? What happened? I could hear Nada's shrieks halfway to town," Teta Lily asked, her eyes darting from one to the other.

"Dragan ..." Miriana spit out between sobs. "I ... I took him his lunch ... " She couldn't finish.

"Miriana, did he attack you?" Teta Lily asked in a sharp tone.

Miriana just nodded.

Teta Lily turned to Stefan. "Go to the mill, please, Stefan. Find Miriana's parents and bring them here," she pleaded. She hadn't finished speaking before Stefan was at the door.

"Miriana, are you okay? I mean, did he hurt you?"

"Just my wrists. And my mouth. He ... he was drunk. He found Tata's plum brandy."

"Oh, Sertse!" She stroked Miriana's hair. "Did he touch you? I mean ..."

Miriana described the scene to her aunt.

Nada was sucking her fist furiously.

"I think Nada's hungry, Teta Lily," Miriana said.

"No doubt," her aunt replied. "I'll have to feed her in a minute, but first I want to look after you."

"I'm all right." She was still shaking, and she felt dirty. "You can nurse Nada," Miriana's lips turned up in a shaky smile that her eyes did not reflect. She took a hanky from her pocket and wiped her face.

"You will never have to see that man again," Teta Lily asserted.

Miriana nodded and sighed.

I'm not going to stay alone with any more soldiers-in-hiding, she thought, *especially this one.*

CHAPTER 12

Repairing a Problem

DRAGAN LEFT IN THE MIDDLE OF THE NIGHT AS HE HAD come. Miriana didn't see him leave, and she was glad not to have to face him. Even though she tried not to think of the incident in the cellar, it crept into her mind, and she felt embarrassed and repulsed.

Except for those memories, May was a happy month for Miriana. Her father had recuperated from pneumonia and resumed his work full time at the mill. Mama seemed more cheerful than Miriana could remember seeing her in a long time. Nada was healthy and a source of joy for everyone—except Zoran. Sometimes he loved the baby, but more often, he showed jealousy for the attention she received. It seemed to Miriana that Teta Lily was busy twenty-four hours a day. She was up at night to nurse the baby, and, during the day, she cleaned and cooked. For that, Miriana was grateful, because it meant she could finish her school year.

On Saturday morning, three weeks after Dragan left, there was a knock on the door early in the morning. Miriana had not even had her breakfast, and Teta Lily was nursing the baby. Zoran was still sleeping, and Miriana's parents had already gone to the mill. Miriana padded to the door in her bare feet, hugging the nightgown to her body with one arm and smoothing tufts of hair with the fingers on her other hand.

She opened the door just a crack at first, and peeked through the narrow opening.

"Mrs. Stefanovich!" she gasped, and yanked the door wide open. "Please come in." Miriana forgot her appearance as she started speculating why Stefan's mother was there at that hour.

Mrs. Stefanovich thanked her quietly. She clutched a hanky to her nose, which she removed only to dab at her red and swollen eyes. She was pale, and there were dark circles under her eyes.

"Is Stefan here?" she blurted.

Miriana shook her head.

"Do you know where he is? He didn't come home last night." Mrs. Stefanovich burst into tears that she fought to control. Miriana stood awkwardly beside her friend's mother and wondered what she should do. She thought about the conversation she had had with Stefan yesterday. She knew he had quarreled with his mother again, and she sympathized with Stefan. His mother wanted him to quit violin now and stay home to look after the farm. Miriana was torn. Mrs. Stefanovich looked miserable.

She really cares, Miriana thought.

Teta Lily removed Nada from her breast and put her into the cradle. She put her arms around Mrs. Stefanovich and guided her to a chair at the table. "Come, Mrs. Stefanovich. Come and have a cup of tea with us. Let us help you."

Miriana, relieved that her aunt was there to help, busied herself making the tea and listened.

"*Bozhe, bozhe*, oh god," Mrs. Stefanovich began again. "I am so worried. If Stefan was out after curfew, he was sure to be arrested."

Miriana stiffened. She hadn't thought of that.

"Let's start at the beginning." Teta Lily tried to calm her. "When was the last time you saw Stefan?" she asked.

"Yesterday morning," Mrs. Stefanovich replied. She sniveled and sighed but stopped crying.

"Miriana," Teta Lily questioned, "was Stefan at school yesterday?"

Miriana nodded. "Yes, we walked home together after school—as least, as far as Chika Rajkovich's place. Stefan had a violin lesson with him after school. That's the last time I saw him."

"Did you check there, Mrs. Stefanovich?" Teta Lily asked.

She shook her head. "No, this is the first place I tried," she replied. "I thought Miriana would be the most likely to know where he is."

"I'll go to Chika Rajkovich's to see if he is there," Miriana volunteered. "You stay here, Mrs. Stefanovich. I'll just get dressed and leave right away."

Miriana jogged all the way to the violin teacher's home. She was breathless when she arrived. She pounded on the door and stood gasping, trying to catch her breath, while she waited for the old man to answer. The door rattled under the pressure of her fist, and a strip of dry, peeling paint rustled as it fell to the ground. Miriana peered at the rest of the house. It was just the same. The fence needed painting too, and the gate hung from only one hinge. The stones on the walk and the narrow driveway at the side of the house had been uprooted from the cement foundation. The windows needed washing, and several of the panes were cracked. Everywhere she looked, she saw neglect. But at least the house was still standing and not blown into a pile of rubble.

Finally, she heard the shuffling of feet, and the door creaked open. Chika Rajkovich stood there in slippers with a housecoat loosely drawn over his pyjamas. His grey-white hair was dishevelled, and his face had a thick, white stubble from ear to ear. He peered at her over the lenses of round glasses perched near the tip of his long, pointed nose, his grey-blue eyes showing no recognition.

"Maestro, it's Miriana Markovich, Stefan's friend. Is Stefan here?" she asked.

"Oh, yes," he drawled, "you came to his lesson a few weeks ago. *Mm, mm.* What's that? What do you want to know?" His breath smelled of garlic and paprika.

"Is Stefan here?" she repeated. "He didn't come home last night, and his mother is looking for him."

"No. No, he's not here. He came yesterday for his lesson. He played badly too. Not like him. He loves that 'Air in G' … but yesterday … anyway, no, he's not here. He left after his lesson as usual."

"Did he say where he was going?" Miriana asked.

"No. No. He seemed a bit upset, but he didn't say anything to me."

"Not even about his violin lessons?"

"Violin lessons? What do you mean?"

"Just that he and his mother quarreled about them again," Miriana answered.

"Oh, that old saw," Chika Rajkovich shook his head.

"I have to go now," Miriana said. "Stefan's mother is worried about him. She thinks he might have been arrested after curfew. Thank you." Miriana turned to go.

"Uh, uh …" The old man held up his index finger as if he wanted to say something but forgot.

"Miriana," she interjected, guessing he had forgotten her name.

"Miriana," he said, and smiled, "please keep me informed. Let me know when you find him."

"Yes, Maestro, I will," she promised. Now she was worried. She couldn't think where else Stefan might be. She had been sure he would be at Chika Rajkovich's. What was she going to tell his mother?

Mrs. Stefanovich was still sitting at the table when Miriana arrived home, panting from running both there and back. She looked up hopefully, but Miriana shook her head. She saw the tears well up in Mrs. Stefanovich's eyes, and she had to drop her head to hide her own feelings.

Miriana felt a rush against her skirt. Zoran clung to both her legs with his arms. "Up, Yanna, up." She reached over and lifted him up into her arms. He squeezed her tightly around the neck, almost cutting off her breath. "I love you, Yanna," he said, and buried his head in the curve of her neck.

The door swung open and crashed shut. Shasula had come to clean.

"Good morning, Mrs. Lily. Morning, Miriana," she sang out in a husky, cheery voice. Shasula's thick mane of hair was flattened and hidden under a bright red kerchief. Her dark eyes were magnified in the smallness of her face, and her voluptuous red lips parted in a wide smile that revealed straight white teeth. Two bracelets jangled on her wrist.

"Zoran! Hi, little man. Do you have a hug for Shasula this morning?" She held her arms out to Zoran who spontaneously reached from Miriana to Shasula, grabbed her, and gave her a big hug. Miriana felt a twinge of jealousy that surprised her and a sense of relief when Zoran wanted to return to her.

"Mrs. Stefanovich, this is Shasula. She helps us in the house when there is something extra to be done," Teta Lily said.

Stefan's mother just nodded.

"Hello, Missus," Shasula responded. "Are you Stefan's mother?"

"Uh, yes," Mrs. Stefanovich replied, haltingly. "Do you know my Stefan?

"Sure," Shasula replied. "I seen him here a few times. In fact, I seen him last night."

Miriana saw Teta Lily start.

"Shasula," Teta Lily said excitedly, "Stefan didn't come home last night, and his mother is looking for him. Do you know where he is now?"

"Sleeping, I guess. At least, he was when I left."

"Sleeping where, Shasula?" Teta Lily persisted.

"At our place. Over at the camp," Shasula replied, with a toss of her head in the general direction.

"Shasula, I think you had better explain," Teta Lily said tersely. Miriana noticed that her lips were drawn into a thin line, and her face was flushed.

"What's to explain?" Shasula replied. She stood with her feet apart, her hands on her hips, her head thrown back. "I met Stefan last night. He was carrying his violin, and I invited him to come to play for us. My brother and a few of his friends fiddle too. So, he came. It was a good time." Shasula stopped and grinned.

"So he stayed overnight at your house? And he's okay?" Mrs. Stefanovich inquired, hugging her soggy hanky between her two hands.

"Last I looked," Shasula said, her hands on her swaying hips. "Say, Mrs. Lily, I'm tired this morning. We went to bed late. Can I get started with the cleaning so that I can get home soon?"

"Yes, sure, Shasula. Go to the pump and get a bucket of water." She turned to Zoran, "Go with Shasula to get water."

Zoran pulled his thumb from his mouth and slid down from his perch on Miriana's lap. "Yah, I gonna help Shas'a get water. You let me pump, Shas'a?"

Shasula took the pail in one hand and Zoran's hand in the other. The door slammed behind them. Teta Lily sighed.

Mrs. Stefanovich stood up. "I … I guess I'd better go and find Stefan. Thank god, he's all right."

"Mrs. Stefanovich, please, would you let me go find Stefan?" Miriana pleaded. "Maybe he needs a little time to himself. He's still upset."

"That's a good idea, Miriana," Teta Lily responded. "Mrs. Stefanovich, why don't you go home and get some rest? You look tired. We'll give Stefan breakfast, and he can come home in a while."

Mrs. Stefanovich nodded. "Thank you. You have both been very kind. I will. His grandparents are worried too, and they will be glad to hear that he is safe." She kissed each of them on both cheeks and turned to leave. Shasula and Zoran nearly knocked her over as she left and they bustled in with their pail of water.

All the way to the gypsy enclave, Miriana kept thinking what she should say to Stefan. It wasn't enough anymore that she commiserated with him. He needed more support than that. Obviously, the situation with his mother wasn't getting better by itself. What's the real stumbling block with Stefan's mother, the time or the money? If only she knew.

What difference would it make, anyway? she thought. She couldn't do Stefan's chores or pay for his lessons. But as she thought it over, an idea started to take shape in her mind.

Miriana spied Stefan leaving one of the houses just as she arrived at the gypsy camp. He was bent over, staring at the path as he skulked along, carrying his violin case under his arm.

"Stefan!" she called and stopped to wait for him. Stefan's head jerked up. There was a look of surprise on his face.

"What … how …?" Stefan stuttered, "Oh, I know. Shasula. She told you." He put his free arm around her shoulders and squeezed gently. Miriana felt a twinge of guilt for having sided with his mother, if only briefly, and she blushed.

Stefan guided her along with his arm, and they strode briskly back in the direction Miriana had come from. "I was so upset when I met Shasula after my lesson; she invited me to come here and play with her brother. I was glad to delay going home. He's one good fiddler, her brother, and he never had a lesson in his life. He plays by ear. He can't read a note. It's not what I am learning. He uses a lot of rubato and slides." He seemed to be hearing the music again in his head. "Anyway, next thing I knew, it was past the curfew hour, and I couldn't go home. So I stayed overnight."

"Yes, your mother came looking for you. I knew you hadn't been home. She was worried about you, Stefan."

"Yeah," he mumbled.

"You know, Stefan, I went to Chika Rajkovich's house to look for you first. I thought you might have stayed there. He's an old man. He has trouble moving, and his place is falling apart." Stefan shot her a puzzled look, but he said nothing so she continued. "The stone walk needs fixing; the house has loose boards everywhere; there's a broken window that lets in the rain; and that's just on the outside. What does the rest of the house that I didn't see look like?"

"Like the outside, I suppose. I can't say I really noticed. I think about other things when I'm there. Why do you bring this up now?" he asked, his voice peaking with curiosity.

"Well, I was just thinking. I wonder if Chika Rajkovich needs some help around his house. Maybe you could work in exchange for your lessons. If it's a question of money, maybe your mother won't object if she doesn't have to pay."

"I ... I don't know," Stefan replied. "Somehow I think the maestro depends on that income, even if it's in the form of food. He's so devoted to the violin that I think he *would* teach me for nothing. But of course, I wouldn't ask him to."

"Well, it was just a thought," Miriana said. She felt deflated. "I was hoping it could solve the problem. Didn't you work for him to pay for the combs you gave me for Christmas?"

"Yes, but that was different," he said. "He didn't need the combs."

They were at the gate to her house. Miriana turned away from Stefan so that he wouldn't see the disappointment that she was sure must be mirrored in her eyes. His arm dropped from her shoulder. "Teta Lily invited you to come for breakfast. You haven't eaten yet, have you?" she asked.

"No, I haven't, but I'm not hungry, thanks. We ate late last night."

"Okay. Bye, Stefan," she said. He was staring off into the distance and didn't answer her. She shook his arm. "Where will you go now? Chika Rajkovich wanted to know when we found you."

"I think I will go to his house now." Stefan shifted his gaze and gave her a faint smile. "Don't worry, Miriana. I'll tell him myself. And ... Miriana ... maybe I'll talk to him about your idea. At least I'll give it some thought. It's a question of time too."

Miriana felt her mouth twist into a reluctant smile. "Okay. Bye, again." The thought of breakfast was appealing now, and she took the steps to the house two at a time.

Life would get better, wouldn't it?

CHAPTER 13

Miriana Loses

I T WAS LATE IN THE MORNING BY THE TIME THE PROBLEM OF Stefan's disappearance was solved. Teta Lily, Zoran and Mama were ready to go to market. Miriana said good-bye to them and sat down to eat the porridge her mother left for her.

This will be a good time to finish my assignment, she thought. *The house will be quiet.*

She finished her breakfast quickly and went to the bedroom to get her book. It was on the little table beside her new bed. Her new bed! Chika Rajkovich had lent them the bed for as long as they needed it.

"How many beds can I sleep in at once?" he had quipped, his soft, narrow eyes gleaming, and his mouth turning up at the corners. When Stefan had told Chika Rajkovich the story of the divided room, without hesitation the old man had offered the furniture to Miriana's family. The next day, Tata had borrowed the cart and the ox to pick it up.

The little table that matched the bed barely fit in the room and pushed at the blanket that divided the room in two.

Strange, Miriana thought, looking around. *I left the combs here this morning.* She dropped to her knees on the wood plank floor and searched under the table and both beds. The sweetish odour of homemade soap wafted from the furniture and floor as she groped around with her hand, feeling for the combs.

They definitely were not there. Miriana plopped on the bed, resting her elbows on her knees. She willed her heart to stop pounding so she could think. Zoran had gone to market, so he couldn't have taken them. She thought back to the hour before breakfast. She could clearly remember changing her mind about wearing them and putting them on the table. No one else would have been in her room except … except Shasula. *She took them!* It wouldn't be the first time she had taken something.

Miriana charged out of the room calling Shasula as she went. She nearly collided with her as Shasula, bent over to the side with the weight of her pail of sudsy water, shuffled out of Teta Lily's room.

"Shasula, my combs. Where are my two hair combs, the glossy ones that have the curved prongs? The ones that Stefan gave me for Christmas?" she blurted out, breathlessly.

Shasula almost dropped the heavy pail, and its contents sloshed around inside the bucket and ran over the edges. "What'er you talkin' about?" she answered saucily, putting her rough, red hands on her round hips.

"I left them on my table." Miriana spoke rapidly, and her heart was pounding again. "They were there this morning when you cleaned the room. What did you do with them?"

"Do with them? I didn't do anything with them, you silly girl." Shasula tossed her long black mane with a haughty flip of her head. "I just clean here. I don't pick up your things."

Miriana stepped deliberately in front of her.

"No, Shasula. I mean, you took them, and I want them back. Give them to me. Right now." Miriana stuck out her hand. She had never confronted anyone before, and her voice quavered.

Shasula dropped her hands to her side. "I have to finish this work before your mother gets home. Besides, I'm tired. You just want to get me in trouble. I didn't touch your combs. You must have lost them while you were playing in the yard." She picked up the heavy bucket and stepped around Miriana, her colourful cotton skirt swirling against her swarthy legs and bare feet.

Miriana grabbed her arm. "Shasula, please!" Her cool grey eyes met Shasula's flashing dark brown eyes but only for a second before Shasula pulled away.

"You *are* a child. What would I want with your combs?" she snapped and padded out the back door, the foaming fragrant water swishing as she went. The door slammed behind her emphatically.

"And you are a *thief*!" Miriana screamed at the slammed door. "All you gypsies are thieves!"

She clenched her fists at her side.

Mama would be disappointed if she thought I was upset over mere things, Miriana thought. *There are so many important issues these days, she would say.*

But Miriana couldn't help herself, and two long tears of anger and self-pity trickled down the sides of her nose.

CHAPTER 14

A Tight Spot
June 1944

Miriana didn't find her combs, not that day or the next. Every time she opened a cupboard or a drawer, she looked for them, but she was always disappointed. The days passed, but she didn't give up hope of finding them. She couldn't tell Stefan they were lost.

"*Schokolade?*" the soldier asked.

Miriana was startled. She and Zoran were returning from a walk to the market, and she hadn't noticed the soldier approach them.

"Oh, yes, please. *Bitte,*" Zoran replied excitedly. His dark brown eyes lit up, and his blond hair flopped as he jumped up and down in front of the soldier.

The soldier asked Zoran a question, and Zoran looked puzzled.

"He's four," Miriana replied, shyly in German, "and I'm sixteen."

She took the chocolate from the soldier and tucked it in her smock pocket. She would enjoy it later.

"Danke," she said to thank him.

Zoran bit hungrily into his.

"Say thank you, *danke,*" Miriana coached Zoran gently.

With his mouth full of sweet, melting candy, Zoran made a muffled reply that made the soldier laugh and rumple his hair.

Miriana took Zoran's smooth hand in hers, and they headed home. The dust rose as their feet kicked at the dry soil of the road. Grapevines hung limply against stucco walls of cottages and geraniums drooped in window boxes. Everywhere the odour of chickens, ducks and pigs was pungent in the sultry, summer air.

"When my daddy comes home from the war, I gonna have chocolate every day," Zoran asserted as he licked the leftovers from his fingers. "We gonna have our own house too."

As they turned into the yard and climbed the stoop to the house, Miriana could hear hushed voices in the kitchen. The talk was of Partisans and Germans. She recognized the voice of Atsa Teshki.

Bad news, she thought.

Zoran dashed ahead of her and threw his arms around his mother. The conversation stopped, and Atsa got up to leave. He was a short, thin man with stringy grey hair that sprung from his head in uneven clumps. Straight, grey eyebrows pulled together in a constant frown, formed a canopy over small eyes, a long pointed nose, and straight, tight lips pressed together. Even though her parents respected this man, Miriana had a hard time seeing beyond his rodent-like features.

Perhaps it's more the news he brings than his nature that I am seeing, she thought.

Miriana looked with inquisitive grey eyes, first at her mother, then at her father. They said nothing, but fear was clearly there on their pale faces. Miriana knew she would just have to wait to find out.

She waited through dinner, through Teta Lily prodding Zoran to go to bed early. Her bedtime came, and there was still no discussion.

The night was hot and sticky. Miriana lay, not sleeping, listening to her parents tossing and turning in the next bed. She felt as if she had only just fallen asleep when she heard them up and in the kitchen.

What time is it? she thought. The room was still dark, and outside there was barely a glimmer of red sun. Earlier than usual, she concluded, even for her father. Then she heard Zoran's voice. *Zoran is up too?* Miriana grabbed her smock and joined the others in the kitchen.

"Mama?"

Her mother came and put her arms around her.

"The soldiers are coming," she whispered. "The Partisans shot a German officer yesterday. In retaliation, the Germans are rounding up a hundred Serbian men and boys to shoot. We have to hide your father and Zoran. I didn't tell you last night because I wanted you to sleep. You have to be strong today."

Miriana froze. Her father? Zoran?

"What did they do? Why?" she asked.

"Come on," her mother said, prodding her gently. "Help your aunt get Zoran dressed. Get dressed yourself."

Miriana changed into her smock. She took Zoran, who was wriggling in Teta Lily's arms. "Come on, Zoran. You are the last one to get dressed!" she said. She tugged a shirt over his head and helped him fasten the buttons on his pants while he giggled and pulled teasingly at her unkempt hair.

Mama put out buns and salami. Her father and Zoran each took a few bites, her father washing his down with a cup of coffee that was mainly chicory.

"Quickly, now, bring Zoran to the cellar," Mama whispered. Miriana swung the little boy into her arms, and the five of them descended the narrow wooden stairs to the cellar.

"Zoran, listen carefully," said Teta Lily. "We will be playing a game like hide-and-seek. You have to stay in here for a while, and you must be still, very still. No talking. Can you do that?" Teta Lily spoke softly and seriously to Zoran, her large hazel eyes pleading with him.

"Okay," he said excitedly.

"Good boy," she replied.

"Whose is gonna find me, Mama?" he asked.

Miriana's father lifted the cover off a large, round, barrel-shaped device, exposing the inside of the drum of the machine they used to comb the wool they sheared off sheep. It was spacious enough for a child to sit in, but not much more. The metal interior was cold and slippery, and it smelled of oil. Tata lifted Zoran into the machine's cavity.

"No, Mama!" Zoran shrieked. His eyes grew wide as he squatted in the machine. He threw out his arms crying. "I don't wanna stay in here. I don't like it. Take me out!"

"Zoran, you *must* stay," Teta Lily begged. Miriana could see that she was fighting tears.

"Zoran!" Miriana interrupted her aunt. "Do you remember yesterday the soldier gave us chocolate? You ate yours right away. Was it good?"

Zoran nodded.

"Well," Miriana continued, "I saved mine. Look, I still have it in my pocket. If you will be a good boy for your mama and me, I will give you mine. But first, you have to play the game. Sit down in the drum."

Zoran stared at her and quietly sat down in the cavern of the machine, cuddling his knitted pig his mama handed to him. "I will sit outside the machine, and I will stay here all the time," Miriana said. "Make sure you are quiet so no one can hear you."

They closed the drum, shutting out light and air.

Miriana's father grunted. "They should not be long," he said.

He opened a cubbyhole behind some shelving that swung out.

They had built the cupboard years ago as a hiding spot for many things but it was never intended for a person. Tata squeezed into the cutout in the stone wall. It was a tight fit. Silently, Miriana's mother closed the door with the shelving.

The waiting began.

Sun streaked red-yellow through the windows. Ducks quacked; a rooster crowed; hens clucked. The barnyard was alive with activity. The house was silent.

Teta Lily looked after Nada and busied herself in the kitchen. Mama worked at the mill as usual. The plan was to set the scene as if the three women worked alone on a daily basis.

Miriana kept her promise to Zoran. She sat by the wool machine, on a round wicker bin, spinning wool on a stick. She lost track of the time as she sat there, worriedly tugging at the stray strands of wool. Her hands quivered, and her stomach was in knots. Her mother's words pounded in her head: "A hundred men and boys to shoot. Zoran. Your father."

The door to the cellar opened, and her aunt called softly, "They're coming."

Miriana heard the trucks first, then the sound of men's voices, and, finally, the boots on the floor above. The ceiling shook with heavy footsteps, and there were crashes and thumps as the furniture was pushed aside and cupboards were thrown open.

Zoran, Zoran, do keep still, Miriana begged silently.

The cellar door banged open, and boots thudded down the stairs. Two soldiers appeared. They only glanced at Miriana and proceeded to overturn anything that looked as if it could be possibly hide a man or child. Miriana kept her hands busy and her eyes on her work so that she wouldn't have to meet their eyes.

"Stand up," one of them ordered her in German, gesturing with his hands. She understood the hand language and reluctantly did as he commanded. The soldier wrenched the lid off the bin she had been sitting on and drew out the raw wool. Miriana watched silently. Her hands trembled, so she hid them under her apron. Her stomach churned.

The other soldier poked away at the cupboard where her father was hiding. Something about it had caught his interest. As Miriana watched him, the dread of the situation suddenly overcame her. Her stomach heaved, and she vomited rancid bread, salami, and chicory-coffee across the floor and on the uniform of the soldier who was checking the wool bin.

The soldier leaped back and began hollering in German. Miriana didn't understand a word, but she knew from the tone he was disgusted and angry. She felt miserable, and she didn't care what he was shouting. She collapsed on the floor, and the soldier went in search of a cloth. His companion turned his attention from the cupboard to help him. They wiped his clothing, ridding him of the vomit but not the stench. As they turned to the staircase, they encountered Teta Lily who was on her way down.

She soothed Miriana and helped her clean up. "It's okay, Sertse," she whispered, "They'll be going soon."

"He was poking at the cupboard, Teta Lily," she whispered back. "I was sure he was going to find Tata. I was so scared. I couldn't help myself."

"You mean you were sick just when they were getting close?"

"Yes."

Teta Lily put her hand on her breast and let out a long, slow breath. "That was lucky," she whispered shaking her head. "That was close too. What about Zoran? Did they suspect anything?"

Miriana shook her head. "He was quiet the whole time."

Upstairs, there was a heavy knock of boots as the soldiers left the house.

They are probably going to check out the mill now, Miriana thought. A few minutes later, Mama tiptoed down the cellar stairs.

"They've gone?" Teta Lily asked.

Mama nodded. "They're next door. I don't think they saw me come in. What happened? One of the soldiers sounded angry, even to me, and I don't speak the language." The reek of vomit told her part of the story, and she remembered the same smell on the soldier.

"I was sick all over him. Mama, can we wash this dress?"

"Not just yet. We have to be sure they won't return. How do you feel?"

Miriana just nodded.

They waited until the soldiers finished searching the neighbours' houses before they opened the cupboard for Miriana's father. He was hot and sweating in the confined space. His face, red from the heat, glistened with perspiration and rivulets of sweat streaked his cheeks, chin, and forehead, but he was alive—this time.

Tata opened the wool machine drum and lifted out Zoran. He was asleep. Teta Lily took her child from him and held him close, rocking him gently and crying.

Miriana wanted to take the chocolate and stomp on it. It had come from the devil.

But she knew she couldn't. Zoran would remember the promise of chocolate when he woke up. She had to keep her word to him because there would be other occasions and other trusts to be kept.

CHAPTER 15

One in a Hundred

THE FAMILY HUDDLED SILENTLY IN THE CELLAR. TETA LILY sat and rocked Zoran. Nada slept in her cradle that they had placed at the top of the stairs. Mama hunched over on the bottom step, her muscular brown hands clasped tightly in her lap. Miriana sat trembling beside her father, her arms wrapped about his shoulders, her head nestled in the curve of his hairy neck. No one spoke. The smell of Miriana's vomit lingered in the air.

They waited in the cellar for fear the soldiers would return. They wanted to be ready for Tata and Zoran to return to their hiding spots if it was necessary.

Miriana lost track of time, but after what seemed like an hour or more, there was a noise upstairs. Miriana's mother signaled to the others that she would go upstairs to investigate, and the others should prepare for hiding. She moved with agility and swiftness for her size.

Maybe it's Stefan, Miriana thought, remembering the other

occasions that he had come to check on them. *Oh, I hope not,* she thought as it suddenly occurred what a risk he would be taking.

They could hear voices upstairs: Mama and a woman. There was a shuffling of feet, and the door to the cellar opened. Miriana could see the feet of a woman clad in sturdy brown shoes of worn leather and the thick hose of a villager. The woman descended carefully, her feet turned sideways to negotiate the narrow steps. Her hand appeared on the wall to steady her, and she carried a sodden hanky that she wrung tightly in her hands. Finally, Miriana could see the face.

Mrs. Stefanovich! God, no, now what? Miriana thought. She jumped up from her seat. Her stomach churned afresh, and the rancid taste of vomit returned to her mouth.

Mrs. Stefanovich wept uncontrollably. She couldn't speak, and Miriana's mother had to give her message to the others.

Mama was crying now too. She put her arm around Mrs. Stefanovich. "The soldiers found Stefan," she said. "They took him away."

"Stefan!" Miriana shrieked. "Tata! What are we going to do? We've got to help him." She shook her father's strong shoulders. He always solved everybody's problems.

Tata shook his head. Tears welled in the corners of each eye. "There is nothing I can do," he said, clasping and unclasping his hands.

"Atsa! Atsa Teshki!" Miriana blurted. "He always knows what's going on. Ask him. He can help."

Mrs. Stefanovich looked at Miriana's father. "Please," she whispered, "you have to help me."

Tata shook his head again. "Believe me, I wish I could," he said, "but I ..." He shrugged, and a sob racked his body. Miriana couldn't ever remember seeing her father cry before.

Mrs. Stefanovich wailed.

Miriana was desperate. She couldn't relinquish control that easily. There was always a solution to every problem.

There has to be a way, she thought. Her body ached. She felt she would have been sick again if there had been anything left in her stomach. She gagged.

Teta Lily gripped Miriana's shoulders and shook her.

"Miriana, get hold of yourself." She gathered Miriana in her arms.

Miriana tensed. The knot in her stomach wouldn't go away. She broke loose from her aunt's embrace and hugged herself.

There didn't seem to be anything to do. Teta Lily whispered in her sister's ear and left quietly. Zoran, awake now with all the commotion, wanted to play with Miriana, but she kept pushing him away. Mama took Nada and Zoran upstairs and invited Mrs. Stefanovich to go with her.

It all seemed unreal to Miriana. She wandered aimlessly through the house, waiting. Waiting for what? She didn't know. She didn't even notice that her aunt had gone until she returned with news. The prisoners would be shot in the town square at five. No one knew anything about Stefan.

"I'm going," Miriana announced.

"No! You can't go!" her mother said firmly. "It will be too much for you."

Miriana clenched her fists and fixed her eyes on her mother. "Yes. Mama, I have to see for myself. Tata, come with me."

Her father looked at her mother. "No, Miriana, no …" he said, not daring to look at Miriana. "You must not go."

It was nearly five o'clock now. Teta Lily supported Mrs. Stefanovich. Miriana felt a sense of urgency take over. Without another word, she turned and bolted out the door, letting it slam behind her. She heard them call her name. Mama called, Teta Lily too. She could hear her father's heavy footsteps behind her, but she closed her ears and ran towards the town square. Ran. As hard and as fast as she could.

She turned and looked, and she could see her father following behind her. But she was young and swift, and she had a head start. She could outrun him.

The town square was already crowded with people. They were pushing against the ring of soldiers, trying to catch glimpses of prisoners who huddled in a large group against a stone building. Sounds of crying and screaming filled the air.

Miriana ran around the crowd of people, trying to find a place where she could break through. Occasionally, she could see a cluster of prisoners: young and old, lumped together, all of them male, all of them Serbian.

Stefan, Stefan, where are you? For an instant Miriana thought she could see his dark, curly hair. *No, that can't be him*, she reassured herself. But who *was* that? Was that Mr. Josich, the teacher? She peered at the sandy-brown hair, the thick handlebar moustache, and the lined face. It was. It was Mr. Josich! *Why him? He helped them with information. Somebody made a mistake, A big mistake. Ruthless, They're ruthless!*, Miriana shuddered and pushed on through the throng. She wanted, needed, to find Stefan.

Above the din of the crowd, she heard German commands. The soldiers raised their guns.

Then she spotted him. He was there.

"Stefan!" Miriana shrieked as loudly as she could.

Stefan turned his head. His dark, glassy eyes widened. "Miriana!" he called back, and tried to dash forward.

The guns fired. Miriana watched as a bullet slammed into Stefan's chest. Another tore through the flesh of his neck, and blood spurted from his body. She watched him slump forward and fall into the pile with the surrounding bodies.

Oh god, Miriana thought, and she closed her eyes. Her body shook uncontrollably, and she sank to her knees.

Tata, where are you? she thought.

She was immobilized as the soldiers continued to fire. The crack of guns hurt her ears, and she covered them with her hands. She couldn't watch anymore.

Why did I come here? she asked herself.

Then she felt the strong arm on her shoulder. Tata. She picked herself up, threw her arms around his bullish neck and hugged him. "Tata, oh Tata," she repeated again and again, burying her head in the crook of his neck so she couldn't see anything. She had no strength, and she slumped against her father.

At last the firing stopped. The air was dusty and dirty, and it smelled of blood and death.

"Come here, little one," her father said. "You've had enough."

"Tata, they killed him. He's here. Did you see him?" For some reason, she couldn't use his name.

Her father nodded.

Chills ran down Miriana's body. She quivered inside and out. Numbness gripped her.

Tata walked her home, his arms supporting her limp body.

"I have to go," he rasped, when they reached the house. "Someone has to help Mrs. Stefanovich. I'll get the ox and cart to take the body home." He was crying. "I'll come back to see you later, Sertse." He squeezed her shoulder, and without looking at her stony face, he lumbered out the door.

Miriana sat numbly, visions of Stefan in her head. Zoran grabbed her, wanting to play. Nada wailed loudly. But Miriana felt nothing, heard nothing. Her mother put out food, but she couldn't eat. She had no sense of time.

It was almost dark when Tata returned. His eyes were dry, but they were red and swollen.

"Stefan's body is at home. We will go tomorrow."

CHAPTER 16

Saying Good-bye

MIRIANA BARELY SLEPT ALL NIGHT. IN THE MORNING, SHE felt tired and tense. Dark circles framed her eyes. Her head was pounding, and her ears were ringing and pulsing. The only thought in her mind was that she was going to say good-bye to her best friend. Perhaps he was more. The memory of the Christmas kiss was tangled and trapped between the crack of gunfire and screams of people.

"Are you sure you want to go?" her father asked.

"Yes, Tata, I'm sure," she replied. *I want to see my friend*, she thought. *I want to see if this horrible thing can be true or if it was just a nightmare.*

Mama stayed home to look after Zoran. Miriana, Teta Lily, and Tata trudged to the Stefanovich farm. The day was hot already, and they sweated in the heat. By the time they arrived, streaks of wet dust dotted their faces.

Miriana stood with her arms clasped tightly across her chest, her head bowed, while they waited for their knock to be answered. A tearful guest opened the door and, in a weepy voice, invited them to come in.

The air in the house was hot and carried with it the acrid odour of candlewicks in the throes of dying out. Sounds of sobbing and sighing filled the house. In the living room, Stefan's old baba sat in her rocking chair, rocking and rocking, and staring into space. Her face was wet with tears, but she made no sound. His grandfather, Deda, sat nearby on a sofa, hunched over and leaning on his cane for support as he sobbed. Here and there, a mourner stood or sat, conversing or crying.

As they entered the room, Mrs. Stefanovich stood up, flung her arms around Teta Lily's neck, and wailed loudly. The two women clasped together, rocking and crying in unison. Miriana's throat felt parched and dry. She felt as if she wanted to vomit but could not; she hadn't eaten anything for two days. If only she could, she thought, she would feel better. Mrs. Stefanovich released Teta Lily and turned to Miriana. Miriana felt her cheek, wet and hot against her own, and felt her body heave with sighs. She put her arms around Mrs. Stefanovich and felt herself become limp and helpless, folding into this woman's warm embrace. How long she clung to her, she couldn't say.

When she finally stood up alone, as Mrs. Stefanovich squeezed her arm and released her, she saw Stefan. He was lying on a board at the side of the room. His body was draped with a piece of black cloth, and only his head was visible. Candles burned at his head and his feet. With slow, deliberate steps, Miriana picked her way across the room, her eyes riveted on Stefan. She put out a hand and touched the bruises on the side of his face. His skin was cold but yielding to her touch. His eyes were closed, and his lashes looked longer than ever. She brushed her hand across his tousled curls, and they sprung back as she released them. A small patch of hair was still matted with blood where his bather had missed washing him.

"Stefan," she whispered gently. There was no answer, no response, and no voice until a single sustained note of the violin cut across the room.

Abruptly, the crying and talking stopped as the high-pitched strings gripped the roomful of people, mesmerizing them. Miriana started and looked up. Chika Rajkovich, his eyes misty, his mouth set in a stubborn grimace, held Stefan's violin tucked under his chin. Captivating sounds of Bach's "Air on the G String" poured from the instrument as the fingers of his left hand gripped the bow, forcing the hairs to slide across the strings, and the fingers of his other hand deftly pressed the strings into the neck of the violin, making them sing.

Oh god, thought Miriana, *that's Stefan's favourite piece*. Pain gripped both her mind and her body. She doubled over, clutching her chest and abdomen with each of her arms. Tears flowed from her eyes, and she shook uncontrollably.

"Stefan, Stefan!" she moaned. Her father grasped her and held her against his burly body.

"Oh, my little girl," he whispered, "I wish it was me, not him. It should have been me. He was so young."

Miriana shook her head and sunk into the comfort of his arms. "No, Tata. No, not you. Not him. Not you, not him. No!"

As the last notes of the air fell from the violin, the sounds of quiet weeping and moaning filled the room once again.

"Come on, let's go home," she heard Teta Lily say.

Miriana felt her aunt's arm leading her firmly towards the door. Miriana's mind was a blur. Nothing made sense to her. She hurt all over.

What is this war doing to our lives? Will it ever end? she screamed in her mind.

She looked at Stefan one last time, tears blurring her vision.

"Good-bye, Stefan."

CHAPTER 17

A Welcome Find

FOR WEEKS AFTER STEFAN'S DEATH, MIRIANA FELT AS IF SHE were living wrapped in a sack. It was a covering woven of memory and hurt that travelled with her everywhere. She ate with it on, she worked with it on, and she even wore it to bed. In the middle of the night, if she turned over, the sack turned with her.

"Stefan is dead," it reminded her.

That was her first thought in the morning and her last thought at night. The day's routine was the same—chores to be done, children to be looked after. She did everything routinely, without feeling, wearing her mourning mantel.

Miriana's grief suffered another setback when she learned that it *was* Mr. Josich she had seen in the square. The school closed after his death. There wouldn't be any more classes while the war was in progress.

What did it matter anyway? Miriana thought. She couldn't concentrate. *And Stefan ...* she sighed. There were others too: Pavlo, Dmitri, Juri, Vladimir.

Near the end of August, Shasula did not come to the house for three days, in spite of the messages Miriana's mother sent asking her to help. She sent Miriana again to the gypsy camp to inquire. Shasula was home and, in her flippant style, reported that she had been sick, but she agreed to come that day.

Something nagged Miriana about the way Shasula looked. There were bruises on her arms and a small cut under her left eye. Miriana had seen the apple-red scarf Shasula was wearing knotted around her head many times before, but today it looked different.

Perhaps it's the way the scarf is tied today, Miriana thought. The billowing white cotton blouse tucked into the fading skirt of many colours with the voluminous square pockets was also familiar. Miriana just couldn't put her finger on it. *Anyway, it's not important,* she decided. *She's coming.*

Miriana spent the morning in the kitchen. She was becoming a competent cook, out of necessity, she decided. She peeled the carrots and sighed. She cut the peppers and sighed. Each time she sighed, it seemed, momentarily, that a burden had been lifted from her chest. Then, like a leaded blanket, it would settle on her body again. She had no appetite for food these days. Many times, she had forced herself to eat only to please her mother or her aunt. When Zoran fixed his eyes on her and watched to see if she was going to eat or not, Miriana felt obligated to at least take a bit. If she didn't, Zoran would cross his arms and refuse to eat.

Miriana was pulled out of her reverie by the sound of her name. Shasula was calling her from the bedroom. "Miriana, give me a hand with this bed, will you? I want to move it over to the side so I can wash the floor underneath." Shasula stood in the doorway, leaning against the frame with her hip.

"Oh, yes, sure," Miriana replied. "Just let me dry my hands first." She concentrated on the towel to avoid having to look directly at Shasula. She didn't want Shasula to see her moist and teary eyes.

The bed, constructed of hardwood dovetailed and glued in a box frame, was heavy. Shasula grabbed the head of the bed and directed Miriana to take the foot. "Let's just move it over here by the curtain so I can get in by the wall," Shasula said, jerking her head towards the curtain.

The two of them heaved and pushed. The bed moved, grudgingly at first, but once it started to slide, they were able to keep it moving across the wood floor until it intruded on the other half of the room, her parents' section.

Shasula straightened and groaned, pressing the flat of her hands against her back and arching in an elongated cat stretch. Her red scarf caught on the hook that held the blanket and rope, yanking it from her head.

Miriana gasped and stared. Shasula was bald! The white skin of her scalp was dotted with uneven tufts of short, coarse, black hair and stubble that reminded Miriana of her father's face when he hadn't shaved for several days.

Shasula scowled, turned, and grabbed the scarf from the hook. Wordlessly, she unknotted it and re-tied it around her head. It hung askew and flat against her skull.

Miriana was too astonished to say anything. She retreated in haste to the kitchen, picked up a carrot and the paring knife, and stood staring out the window into the yard. She could hear the swish of water as Shasula washed the floor. The sweetish smell of soap overpowered the delicate aroma of the vegetables Miriana was peeling.

Why? Why did she do it, Miriana asked herself. Shasula had had beautiful hair, and she had been proud of it. She remembered how Shasula used to toss her mane like a wild filly. *Maybe she didn't do it herself,* she thought. The hair had been shaved, not cut. It was irregular, as if there had been a struggle. That would account for the bruises and cuts.

The door smashed. Miriana jumped. Zoran charged across the room.

"You finished yet, Yanna? You gots some more scraps for the piggies and the chick-chicks? They's still hungry." He wiped his sweaty brow with the palm of his hand, and a black streak took shape across his forehead. A trickle of snot dribbled onto his upper lip, and he sniffed twice, trying to suck it back into the cavity of his nose. When that failed, he wiped his nose with his hand, and a second black line appeared across his face above his mouth.

Before Miriana could answer, Shasula dropped the bucket with a thud on the floor, and both Miriana and Zoran started. Shasula hiked up her skirt with one hand and picked up the pail with the other. Limping with the weight of the load, she headed for the door.

"Hi, Shas'a," Zoran called out cheerfully, his little face screwed up. He cocked his head to one side and said, "Shas'a, you look funny. What that on your head?"

Shasula slammed the bucket on the floor. She spun around, put her hands on her hips and leaned forward, glowering at Zoran.

"It's my scarf, you ninny."

Miriana bristled. She felt Zoran's hand slide into hers.

"You don't look so good yourself," Shasula added. "When's the last time you looked in a mirror?" Then she softened, and her shoulders slumped. "Come on, I'll wash you off under the pump." Shasula jerked her shoulder towards the door, beckoning Zoran to accompany her.

"Come, Zoran," Miriana said, bending over to his height. "I'll bring the scraps for the animals, and after you have washed, you can take them."

"You coming too, Yanna?" Zoran asked.

Miriana nodded, squeezing his hand. She stood up and poured the peelings into the slop pail for Zoran.

Shasula washed Zoran, and Miriana sent him off with his peelings. As soon as he was out of earshot, Miriana grabbed Shasula by the arm.

"He's only little! How could you talk to him like that?" she hissed at Shasula. "He doesn't know how to be coy. He was just being honest."

Shasula shook her arm free of Miriana.

"What happened to you, anyway?" Miriana persisted.

Shasula threw back her head and burst into laughter, though she didn't sound happy. It sounded more like mocking. Her free hand rested haughtily on her hips

"What? Don't tell me you don't know," she said, between ripples of derisive laughter that shook her body. "Surely your mama or your auntie told you."

Miriana stared blankly at Shasula. What was she laughing at? *How unpredictable this girl is*, Miriana thought.

Shasula was suddenly quiet. She peered at Miriana from under her red kerchief that had slipped down her forehead. "You really don't know, do you?" she said.

Miriana shook her head.

"Oh, what an innocent babe you are," Shasula said, rolling her eyes. "Well, I'll tell you. The good people of this town shaved my head because I had a German boyfriend. A lover." She crossed her arms. Her brow furrowed, and her lips pouted. "What business is it of theirs? They wanted to 'teach me a lesson.' 'Collaborating with the enemy' they called it. Huh. I didn't ask for this damn war."

Shasula stopped. Miriana stared off into space.

"I know who it was," Miriana whispered. "It was Kurt, wasn't it? The one who used to come here with Hans to ask my aunt to translate."

Shasula nodded. "Yeah," she replied. "Now he's gone, and my hair's gone." She shrugged. "Anyway, I'm finished work, now. I'll put this pail away, and I'll be on my way. When the floor is dry, your father can push back the bed."

Miriana looked away. What could she say? She had her own sorrow. "Yeah, okay, I'll tell him," she said softly, and trudged into the house.

Without really thinking what she was doing or where she was going, Miriana wandered to the bedroom door and leaned against the frame. Out of the corner of her eye, she spied something ivory on the night table.

She stared. *Was it? Could it possibly be …?* She dashed over to the table, holding her breath. Miriana squealed with delight. It was. It really was! With gentle, trembling hands, she picked up the combs and cradled them in her palms. *God, oh god, Shasula must have put them here. The combs Stefan gave me for Christmas.*

She remembered the moment he had given them to her. If she closed her eyes, she could remember the warmth of his hands as he handed her the combs and the sound of his voice as he wished her "Happy Christmas." She could imagine the kiss. She squeezed the combs gently between her fingers. Her trembling lips spread into a wide, gentle smile. It was the first time she had smiled inside since his death.

CHAPTER 18

Techa Ivan
Spring 1945

S EVENTEEN, ALMOST EIGHTEEN, MIRIANA THOUGHT AS SHE hurried to get ready to leave. *The last time I went to the train station was almost four years ago.*

She buttoned her red dress. It was tight, and the buttons strained at the bodice as she fastened them. Even that was the same as last time. Her body was fuller and rounder, and her breasts were obvious. Even in her face, there were subtle changes that made her look almost eighteen.

Maturity is such an indefinable thing, she thought.

"Miriana, are you ready?" Teta Lily called from the kitchen.

"Yes, coming, Teta Lily."

Peace! How we rejoiced when the news of the end of the war had come, Miriana remembered as she fastened her shoes. Every day, Teta Lily went to the Red Cross centre to seek news of Miriana's uncle, Techa

Ivan, and finally it had come. She would never forget that day. Teta Lily had come sprinting home, clutching a piece of paper, laughing and crying at the same time. Tears streamed down her cheeks, and her body shook with laughter. She had whirled around the room, first with Zoran in her arms and then with Nada. She had hugged Miriana too, leaving her breathless.

"Miriana!" Mama called this time, bringing Miriana back to the present. She yanked on her sweater and bounded out the bedroom door. "Here I am, Mama."

Her mother was sitting, rocking Nada. She would stay home with the little girl while Miriana, her father, Teta Lily, and Zoran went to meet the train that was bringing Techa Ivan home.

Teta Lily was quiet all the way to the station. She still looked more like a peasant than the elegant lady from the city, Miriana noticed. Her skin was tanned and her hands calloused. She wore the same simple cotton black skirt and white blouse that had hung limply on her frame since the birth of Nada.

But she's still beautiful, thought Miriana. *And smart.*

The train station was packed with people. Farmers, children and women milled around on the platform in tight knots, their bodies brushing against one another as they moved.

How will we ever find Techa Ivan in this crowd? Miriana thought. *I wonder if I would even recognize him if he is with just one other soldier getting off the train. Why, it must be more than five years since I have seen him.*

The train announced its arrival with a whistle before it was visible. The welcome sound triggered an outburst of voices, crying and laughing, that rose in pitch as the train pulled into the station.

It was impossible to get close to the train. They were locked into the crowd like pieces in a giant jigsaw puzzle. They could only watch as soldiers descended from the steps of the train, some leaping, some leaning on others, some carried. As each one appeared, Miriana stood on tip-toe, stretching her body and poking her head left and right, straining to see.

Could that be him? she asked herself of at least four soldiers. It was hard at that distance, in that crowd, to see a face clearly.

Suddenly Miriana heard her aunt shriek. "*Ivan!*" she shouted in a distressed voice. Teta Lily sobbed and tried to push her way through the crowd.

Miriana looked back to the train. A tall, lean man in battledress, his head bowed, picked his way down the metal steps of the train. He moved deliberately, leaning on the arm of a comrade for support as he took one step, leaned, and took another.

Techa Ivan? Miriana's heart thumped. The soldier was missing a leg. *Oh, poor Teta Lily. No wonder she's upset*, Miriana thought. She wanted to reach out to her aunt, to hug her, but Teta Lily had already forced herself forward in the cluster of people.

It's all right, Teta Lily, she wanted to say. *At least he's alive.* She thought of Stefan then. It still hurt. She clutched Zoran's hand tightly, as if somehow clinging to a person kept him safe.

Teta Lily was out of sight. Miriana, Tata and Zoran watched as the soldiers continued to arrive. Miriana was startled when her father raised both arms high above his head, jostling her with the movement. "Ivan," he shouted, in his deep voice.

A soldier on the ladder of the train looked up.

Could this be Techa Ivan? Miriana thought. *Then who was the other man?* Her father continued to wave and shout until the man on the steps looked his way and waved back.

The crowd was re-forming as families fought their way to be together. The man who had waved back pushed his way to them. He grabbed Miriana's father, hugged him, and planted the traditional three kisses on alternating cheeks.

"Nikola," he shouted. Miriana looked at the soldier closely.

Yes, this could be Techa Ivan, she thought, *but how thin he is*. His skin was pale, his whisker stubble tinged with grey, his eyes rimmed with red. And he reeked of tobacco. This was not the handsome man Miriana remembered.

"Where's Lily?" the man asked. Before Miriana's father could answer, he spied Zoran, who stood quietly, his eyes round and fixed on the soldier. "My son?" he asked. "My little Zoran?"

He bent over and picked up Zoran in the crook of his arm. His eyes filled with tears. Zoran reached out for Miriana, but she backed away so that he would have to stay with his father. Zoran showed no recognition of his father, and he seemed to be pleading with Miriana with his eyes to escape the strange man's embrace.

The man noticed her now. "Miriana?" He put his free arm around her shoulders and hugged her.

"Techa Ivan?" She felt the tears come, and she wiped them away with the back of her hand.

"Lily," Miriana heard her father murmur as he jerked his head in the direction of her aunt who was pushing her way back through the crowd. Teta Lily flung herself at Ivan, throwing both arms around his thin body and Zoran.

Miriana held out her arms to Zoran, and he fell heavily into her embrace, clinging to her. He hadn't said a word since the train arrived, and his eyes were still large and round.

Poor little guy, Miriana thought. *He has even less memory of this man than I do.* She hugged him tightly against her, swaying and rocking.

Teta Lily was smiling, laughing and crying in Ivan's arms. He held her quietly, saying only her name. The others waited in silence. As Miriana watched, she thought again about the last time she had come to the train station. It had marked a big change in her life. How close she had come to Teta Lily and Zoran in these past years. They, and Nada, were an important part of her life now. What a comfort it was to hug her aunt when she felt sad about Stefan. How exciting it had been to discuss books, travel, music, life, and university in the city with her aunt. What laughter Zoran had brought into her life.

She kept glancing at the man who was hugging her aunt. He made her feel uneasy, but she couldn't quite decide how or why.

"Come on," Teta Lily said. "Let's go home."

Home, thought Miriana. *What would "home" be like now?* she wondered.

CHAPTER 19

After the War

As if the little house were made of elastic, it accommodated yet one more person. Zoran and Nada slept in the little sitting room off the kitchen, and Techa Ivan moved into the bedroom with Teta Lily. Sometimes, at night, Miriana would hear their muffled voices as they whispered in the dark. She would lie awake, listening to their soft laughter and quiet sobs. Other nights, she would wake up to the sounds of her parents on the other side of the curtain. Sometimes she felt overwhelmed and buried her head in her pillow until the house was silent. She wished desperately that she might have her own room again.

During the day, Teta Lily was so busy with the children, the house, Techa Ivan, and her frequent trips to town that she hardly had time for Miriana anymore.

Techa Ivan sat for long hours, smoking silently and staring off into the distance. When he didn't have cigarettes, he fidgeted with matches and raked the ashtray for butts. He rarely spoke, except when Teta Lily was present to draw him into the conversation. Occasionally he took Zoran on his knee, and Miriana could see Zoran squirm. After only a few moments, he would find an excuse to get down. When Miriana encountered Techa Ivan by herself, she felt awkward. She had fond memories of him from the days when she was a little girl, but she didn't know this strange man who was living in their house. She wondered what he was thinking when he sat contemplatively, saying nothing, seeing nothing. Was he remembering his family, his brother and his parents? The news from the Red Cross had not been so happy for him. His parents and brother were reported as killed in Auschwitz, a German concentration camp.

Techa Ivan was not well. Miriana could see that. He wasn't strong enough to work, and it seemed as if his mind was as weak as his body. Sometimes she would hear him cry out in the middle of the night. Miriana was unsure of her feelings towards him. They seemed to be a blend of fear, pity, and affection from the past. Her heart twisted whenever she saw him.

Without school, Miriana found herself at loose ends. She spent the extra free hours with Nada and Zoran. Nada, close to the age Zoran was when he first came, was talking and walking. It was *her* chubby little hand that nestled trustingly in Miriana's when it was time to feed the animals.

Two months after Techa Ivan's arrival, Teta Lily called Miriana and her parents into a huddle in the kitchen. The children were in bed.

"Ivan and I have made plans," she said, "and we want to discuss them with you."

Miriana sat uneasily on the edge of her chair.

"We have been in touch with a friend in Belgrade," Teta Lily continued. "Dr. Stimach is helping us find a home, and he has found a job for Ivan."

Miriana's mother listened and nodded. "Yes, this is good news! I am happy for you. When are you leaving?"

"We can get seats on the train this Thursday. That's in three days," Teta Lily said.

Miriana started. So many thoughts crammed her head all at once. Her room. She would have her room back. And then, feeling guilty about her selfish thought, her emotions flipped. She knew the departure had to come, but still, it was a shock. In three years, she had adapted to a new life, and now the bottom was falling out. Again.

"That's just enough time to get packed," Teta Lily added. She turned to Miriana's father. "Nikola, can you arrange for a cart for the luggage for us?" She paused and laughed softly. "Not that we have much," she said.

Nikola nodded.

The room was silent. Techa Ivan sat quietly smoking, letting Lily do all the talking. The air was grey-blue, and it stung Miriana's nose and throat as she breathed in the pungent smoke.

Teta Lily took a deep breath. "But there's one more thing: Militsa, Nikola, when we get established, we want Miriana to come to stay with us so that she can get an education."

Miriana tensed.

Does she really mean it? she thought. She looked then at Techa Ivan. He looked back at her and nodded. She looked at her aunt. Teta Lily had her eyes fixed on Miriana's father, knowing he would be the biggest hurdle. Miriana glimpsed at her father. He sat hunched in his chair, wringing his hands and staring at the floor. He was silent.

"She will attend university in Belgrade," Teta Lily continued. "Nikola, you know she is a bright girl, and there is nothing much for her here. The change after the trauma of these last few years will be good for her."

There still was no answer.

"We will take good care of her."

Silence.

Oh, please, Tata, please. I want to go, Miriana pleaded in her mind.

She was wary of voicing her thoughts. She didn't want to hurt her father's feelings.

"Militsa, please, I know she's your only child, and it's hard to let go. But times have changed. Let her come," Teta Lily begged her sister.

"Militsa, Nikola, I agree to this," Techa Ivan said unexpectedly, his deep voice husky from inhaling cigarette smoke.

Slowly, deliberately, Miriana's father nodded.

"Oh, Tata," Miriana exclaimed, "thank you!" She ran to her father and kissed the bald spot on his bowed head. She raced to embrace her mama and her aunt, and then, hesitantly, she approached Techa Ivan and planted a kiss on his cheek. He smiled at her, and, for a second, Miriana had a glimpse of the uncle she remembered as a little girl.

Miriana felt herself soften and relax. She felt as if the tension of the past few months was flowing out her fingertips and toes and the roots of her hair. A ray of sunshine broke through her cloud of uncertainty and grief.

CHAPTER 20

Her Own Room

Miriana stood in the middle of her room, her own room. The little window was pushed open, and a gentle May breeze carried the fresh scent of new growth and the quiet whirr of the mill.

The room was the same as before, with her bed, dresser, and night table, but everything felt different. Teta Lily, Techa Ivan, Zoran and Nada were gone. The war was over.

Miriana thought about the past three years, how hard they had been. She thought about Atsa, Dragan, and Josif; the kindly doctor, the birth of Nada; and the scare over losing her father and Zoran. Most of all, she thought about Stefan.

She looked in the mirror. Some strands of hair had come loose from the pins that held her hair in a roll. That, at least, had not changed. She stabbed a few more pins in her hair to hold the loose ends in place. Then, with gentleness, she picked up the combs Stefan had given her.

This comb is happiness, she thought, as she pushed in the first one.

It's my opportunity to start a new life in Belgrade with Teta Lily and her family and an opportunity for education. And this is my sad comb, she thought, as she placed the second one in her hair. *This one reminds me of my best friend, my friend who wanted this opportunity for both of us, who won't be there to share it with me.*

Together, the combs made a pair.

She smiled at her reflection in the mirror as a tear rolled down her cheek.

CPSIA information can be obtained at www.ICGtesting.com
Printed in the USA
LVOW11s0412101014

408100LV00001B/11/P